GRIZZLE'S

ST ~~GRIZELDA'S~~

SCHOOL

FOR GIRLS,

GOATS AND
RANDOM BOYS

STRIPES PUBLISHING
An imprint of the Little Tiger Group
1 The Coda Centre, 189 Munster Road,
London SW6 6AW

A paperback original
First published in Great Britain in 2017
Text copyright © Karen McCombie, 2017
Illustrations copyright © Becka Moor, 2017

ISBN: 978-1-84715-776-8

Printed and bound in the UK.

2 4 6 8 10 9 7 5 3 1

PROPERTY OF:

ST GRIZZLE'S,
SCHOOL FOR GIRLS

Kindly on loan to

NAME	YEAR
Bertha Huggit	1926
Trinny Winterbottom	1953
Flossie Fitzgibble	1962
Arabella Crump	1998

Chapter 1

Too Many Bums for One Girl

And some big changes...

I've been staring at penguins' bums
for quite a long time now.

On the TV, I mean – we don't have
any real, live, fishy-breathed ones flip-flapping
about in the living room or anything.

I know staring at penguins' bums might sound
kind of fun, but fun things turn into boring things
when you do them too often. And we stare at
penguins' bums A LOT in our house.

It's cos my mum's a zoologist. You'd THINK
that'd mean exciting stuff, like she'd take me to
hang out with pygmy hippos or stroke jaguars or
stingrays or ocelots or something.

But no. It's all about endless film clips of
penguins, penguins, penguins and their bums,
bums, bums, just cos Mum's doing this important
project thingammee about how they waddle or
something.

"...so, Dani, that's when my boss told me..."

Mum is saying as she kneels in front of the TV, her eyes glued to the widdle-waddling birds, "...I mean, it's always so difficult to get funding..."

I know this sounds bad, but I sort of switch off when Mum's talking about her work. Especially right now, since my best friend Arch will be here any minute and I've been daydreaming about what we've got planned for the afternoon.

"...such an amazing opportunity..." Mum carries on, though I think I might have missed a bit. OK, a lot. "...it'll mean big changes, of course, but..."

I sit fidgeting on the sofa, twisting the head of my Tyrannosaurus rex (plastic one, not real – duh!). The thing is, I'm not that interested in any big changes happening at Mum's work. I don't mean to sound rude – I bet Mum wouldn't exactly find it fascinating if I told her they're laying new floor-tiles in the smelly boys' toilets at school.

And it's not just me – my dog Downboy is fidgety, too. Normally he loves "**ARF! ARF! ARF!**"ing at any random animals that pop up on telly, but today he's had enough of penguins and is entertaining himself by licking my knees through the holes in my skinny jeans instead.

I wonder how much longer Arch'll be, I think to myself, as I stop nibbling the end of one of my messy plaits long enough to shove Downboy away. (He comes straight back and starts eating the laces on my beat-up trainers.)

Then all of a sudden – right in the middle of a waddle – Mum finally presses pause on the remote control.

The penguins on screen freeze like they're playing a game of big-bummed Statues.

"So?" says Mum, turning and looking at me expectantly.

"So ... that was great," I reply, flashing Mum my best pretend ooh-that-was-interesting! smile as I scramble up off the sofa.

"Er, glad you enjoyed it," says Mum, sounding a bit confused. "But more importantly, what do you reckon, Dani?"

"Huh?" I mumble vaguely, hovering halfway to standing.

What is Mum on about? Whatever it is, she'd better tell me quick, cos Arch is arriving any minute to make our latest mini-movie. It's our thing. We got into doing mini-movies after we found these totally funny clips on YouTube. Some little kid's parents got hold of his toy dinosaur collection and made films with them when he was asleep. They had the dinos doing stuff like watching *Toy Story* with teeny bowls of popcorn or all piling on his blue plastic scooter and zooming across the dining-room floor.

The clips were so cool, we decided to make our OWN films with a bunch of random ex-toys we didn't play with any more, plus some extras from the local charity shop. Between us we have forty-six. They are:

- 9 Beanie Boos
- 8 dinosaurs
  (all kinds, but my favourite is the T rex)
- 8 teddies (various sizes)
- 7 LEGO figures
- 5 Barbies
- 4 Star Wars characters
  (Chewbacca, Yoda, R2-D2 and a
  one-armed Stormtrooper)
- 2 Furbys (broken/silent)
- 2 Elmers
- 1 unicorn (tiddly)

We used to have TWO unicorns, but Downboy ate the big one in the middle of a Doctor Who scene me and Arch were filming, which was pretty annoying, since it took AGES to tape the rounded bit of an egg box to the big unicorn's head and turn it into Strax the Sontaran. We recast using a small teddy – moulding a Sontaran domed head out of Play-Doh since Downboy had eaten the rest of the egg box. We stuck it up on YouTube and it got the most views we've ever had – one hundred and three.

Our best total before that (sixty-nine views) was for our One Direction music vid, which starred Chewbacca as Harry Styles.

"Dani...?" Mum says, with a little uncertain frown on her forehead.

"Uh-huh?" I mutter, suddenly sure I just heard a car door shut. Fingers crossed it's Arch getting dropped off by his dad. I can't wait to get started on today's mini-movie – we're studying the Anglo-Saxons in class so we've decided to film a battle. It's going to star the Beanie Boos as Viking invaders and the teddies as Saxons.

"Dani!" barks Mum, like she's trying to get my attention. "I said, what do you reckon to my news?"

Mum is smiling hopefully at me.

Hopefully I will give her an answer that makes sense, since I wasn't really listening.

I mean, there was stuff about 'in the wild' and 'big changes' at work or whatever.

And before that, I heard something that sounded like, "Blah, blah, **RESEARCH**, blah, **PENGUINS**, blah, blah, **OPPORTUNITY**, blah, blah, **EXPEDITION**, blah, blah, **THREE**, blah, **MONTHS**, blah, blah."

"I reckon," I say warily, "that it's … good?"

Mum breaks into a huge grin.

Yesss! By total fluke, I said the right thing.

"Dani Dexter – come HERE!" she calls out to me, her arms wide.

Uh-oh.

She said something important, and I MISSED it.

Panicking a little bit, I let myself be squished by an enormous hug and pat Mum worriedly on the back with the dinosaur I'm still clutching.

"You are the BEST, most FANTASTIC, most UNDERSTANDING daughter a mother could ever have. You know that, don't you?" Mum murmurs into the side of my head.

BING-BOINNNNGGGG! goes the doorbell, before I get a chance to figure out what she's on about.

"**ARF! ARF! ARF!**" barks Downboy, hurtling into the hall and launching himself at the front door with a dull thud and a scrapetty racket of claws.

Downboy jumps up at stuff all the time. And he chews EVERYTHING, especially things he's definitely not meant to, like shampoo bottles, passports and wasps.

When he was a puppy we took him to dog training classes, but he kept jumping up at all the other owners and chewing the trainer's notes, and Mum was too embarrassed to take him any more.

Mum also gets embarrassed when people ask what kind of dog Downboy is and I say a Box-a-Poo. Or a Poo-Box. But that's what he is – his curly fur is cos he's part poodle and his big smiley mouth is the boxer in him.

"Downboy! Get DOWN!" Mum yells, her lovely, mother-daughter-Tyrannosaurus cuddle moment spoiled.

Phew.

"I'll go – it'll be Arch," I tell her, wriggling free and racing off.

I shake my T rex in front of Downboy's nose and, as soon as he's distracted, I squish around him and tug the door open.

"Hey!" says Arch, tossing his floppy fringe out of his eyes.

He's holding a small blue backpack, stuffed

with his random ex-toys. I have the same one in red for mine.

"Hey!" I say back to Arch, whipping the dinosaur out of Downboy's reach and waving it in the air to keep him entertained.

Then something peculiar happens. As Downboy leaps

and jumps at me, I don't even try to push him away. That's cos I've JUST remembered another chunk of Mum's one-sided conversation. She said something about me being 'bored in school'. Why would she say that, I wonder...? What exactly did I miss back there?

"You OK, Dani?" asks Arch, grabbing Downboy by the collar.

"Er... I've just got to check something," I reply, then turn and pad back towards the living room, with Arch and my overexcited dog following behind.

I have a question that needs answering. Urgently.

"Mum – can you say all that stuff again?" I ask.

Mum is crouched down in front of the TV, ejecting the penguin DVD. She frowns up at me and I realize it's cos I still have my hand – and

19

T rex – in the air. (Oops.)

I lower them both quickly, and accidentally thunk Downboy on the head with the dinosaur. (Oops again.)

"Which part?" says Mum, getting to her feet and waving hello at Arch. "The bit about Professor Green's study into the physiology of penguins' gait?"

I blink, my fuzzy brain trying to translate.

"You mean, how penguins waddle?" I check with her, thinking of Mum's tall, round-tummed boss, who's studied penguins for so long he's starting to look an awful lot like one.

"Yes, 'how penguins waddle', Dani," she answers, rolling her eyes. "Is that the bit? Or the part about Professor Green dropping out of the three-month expedition to Antarctica and me taking his place?"

"Wow!" I hear Arch say.

"What?" I squeak.

My stunned response is so weedy and weeny that Mum doesn't hear above the sound of Downboy yapping and Arch wowing. Anyway, she's just leaned over to click the space bar on the open laptop.

"Or are you talking about the boarding school you're going to?"

Wait a minute – 'bored in school' = '*board*ing school'?

I stare at the website that has popped up on Mum's laptop screen. Arch mooches over to stare, too.

"St Grizelda's School for Girls," he reads.

Jaunty, plinky-plonky music is playing and there is a big photo of lots of smiling girls in grey skirts (SKIRTS!) and straw hats (HATS?!), standing around a snooty grey stone statue of someone I suppose is St Grizelda.

But I can't concentrate on that because a panicky voice in my head is shouting...

Three months?

Boarding school?

THREE MONTHS!

BOARDING SCHOOL!

Chapter 2

Granny Viv to the Rescue (I Hope)

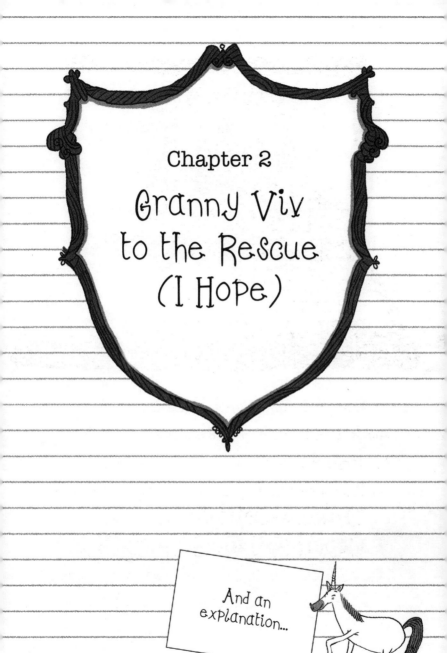

And an explanation...

My mum loves penguins' bums more than me.

Otherwise she'd NEVER dump me in some stuffy old school forever. (OK, three months, which is practically forever, isn't it?)

The school I go to now is not perfect. But at least...

a) it's near home

b) it doesn't have a stupid, stiff uniform, and

c) Arch sits at the table right next to me.

I don't want to go to some super-smart, fancy-pants, dull-grey-skirt-and-silly-hat-wearing boarding school. I don't want to go to a school with no Arch in it.

"Ah, you weren't listening the first time, were you, Dani?" says Mum, spotting that I'm in shock.

I guess it's a bit like the time she said, "Blah, blah, **ROOM**, blah, **TIDY**, blah, blah, **DONATIONS**, blah, OK?" and I said, "Mmm," cos I was busy watching *The LEGO Movie* on DVD.

The next Saturday I felt totally sick when I saw my old rainbow-striped piggy bank, Star Wars lightsaber and *Diary of a Wimpy Kid* book collection on the Kids' Toys table at the school jumble sale. I had to use all the pocket money I'd brought along to buy them back.

"Dani? Huh? I mean ... wow!" Arch burbles uselessly, as he flops down on to the sofa next to Downboy.

Only now it's a sad-sounding "wow", since my best friend has just realized that BOARDING SCHOOL equals me being AWAY.

AWAY from him and from our random ex-toy film project.

AWAY from school and here and home.

AWAY from Mum and Downboy and Granny Viv, of course.

Wait a minute. Granny Viv!

Of course!

"Granny Viv could look after me," I yelp, since THIS IS AN EMERGENCY.

"Er, no, she couldn't," says Mum with a little laugh, as if I'd suggested living with wolves.

I frown a serious "why not?" at her.

"Dani, I barely trust her to look after **HIM**," says Mum, pointing at Downboy, who is crunching snackily on the remote control.

I feel my face go prawn pink and angry.

Mum has a thing about Granny Viv. It's mostly to do with the way she dresses, I think. My neat-freak Mum is embarrassed that her own mother lives in baggy jumpers, leggings and trainers, refuses to own an iron and dyes her hair something called Manic Panic Pillarbox Red.

"For goodness' sake, your grandmother is not a responsible person," Mum says to me now with a weary sigh.

OK, so maybe this isn't ONLY about the way

Granny Viv dresses.

I bet right now Mum is thinking about the time when I was eight and Granny Viv looked after me one Saturday while Mum was at a conference. She gave Granny Viv a very strict schedule which included a visit to a library and helping me with my model rainforest project.

Instead, Granny Viv took me to see her friend Eric play a lunchtime set of punk songs in a pub by the canal. (I liked it. I mean, the songs were a bit shouty, but Granny Viv bought me a packet of crisps and two Cokes while I worked on my project, which was nice.)

Mum was hyper-cross when she found out. And I thought her head might EXPLODE when Granny Viv told her we'd somehow, sort of, maybe managed to leave the project – a cardboard box with papier mâché toucans and sloths – on the number twenty-three bus on the way home...

"Anyway, your gran's studio flat is tiny, so you couldn't move in with her, even if she **WAS** reliable..." Mum carries on with her unfair reasoning.

"Yeah, but Granny Viv could move in here while you're away," I reason right back at her, ignoring the stuff about Granny Viv being non-reliable.

"Look, **NO ONE** can be here while I'm away, Dani," Mum says matter-of-factly. "The local builder's had a cancellation and can come and fit a new kitchen and bathroom for us while the place is empty and—"

"Yoo hoo!" a familiar voice calls out from the direction of the front door.

Yay! It's Granny Viv – she's come to my rescue! (Even if she doesn't know it yet.)

"**ARF! ARF! ARF!**" barks Downboy, leaping off the sofa to go and meet her.

I feel like doing the same.

"Ha! What a welcome!" I hear Granny Viv say, just before she appears in the living-room doorway with a red-lipped smile as bright as her hair.

But the smile slips and Granny Viv's eyes narrow as she sniffs out trouble.

"What's up?" she asks, folding her arms across her chest, jangling all the colourful Indian bangles on her wrists.

"Mrs Dexter's sending Dani to **BOARDING SCHOOL!**" Arch bursts out before I can.

"She's what? Over my dead body!" growls Granny Viv, stepping forwards and wrapping her slightly wrinkly arms around me.

For the second time in five minutes, I'm squashed in a hug.

This time I end up with fluffy purple wool all tickly in my nostrils, as well as a wet hand (Downboy has joined in by nuzzling my fingers and drooling on them).

"Calm down and let me explain!" Mum says. "Today at work I was offered the chance to step in last minute on this amazing expedition to Antarctica. I couldn't say no and, since I leave in two weeks, I've had to arrange everything super quickly."

"Arranging to send Dani to boarding school, you mean? Staying with me isn't good enough?" growls Granny Viv.

But you know something strange?

Even though Mum and Granny Viv are
launching into a proper grumbly, grumpy
argument, I decide everything will be all right.

Cos there is no way Granny Viv will let
me go to stupid St Grizelda's School for Girls.

Will she?

I try to cross my fingers, but that's quite hard

to do when you're...

a) still locked in a tight Gran Hug, and

b) holding a T rex with one hand and trying to push your dog's jaws away from your T rex with the other.

Chapter 3
Welcome to Weirdness

And a Very Scary Thing...

It's Monday morning. The gloomiest Monday morning ever.

A week ago, I thought the hardest thing I had to do was make seventeen weeny swords out of lolly sticks and tinfoil for the Vikings versus Saxons mini-movie.

I had no idea that today I'd be doing something MUCH harder.

Harder than realizing – aged four – that flushing my pet goldfish down the toilet so he could have an adventure meant he was never coming back.

Harder than seeing my mum's face after I cycled into a wall last summer and chipped my front tooth. (Arch says it looks cool, though.)

And that MUCH harder thing was saying goodbye to Granny Viv...

Granny Viv hugged me SO tight as I was

leaving that I still have the imprint of her chunky necklace in my cheek, even though me and Mum are now in the car and miles from home, almost at my stupid new school.

And you know, I can still hear Downboy's whimpers … but that's probably cos he's lying asleep and dreaming in the boot, using my backpack as a pillow.

By the way, it wasn't hard to say goodbye to Arch this morning because he didn't come and see me off like he was SUPPOSED to. Instead his dad rang Mum and told her we should look on the doorstep.

I dashed outside in time to hear a screech of tyres and spot Arch's dad making a quick getaway in their Ford Focus with Arch in the passenger seat. I think the hardest thing for Arch was saying goodbye to me … at least I'm guessing that's why he ducked out of sight when he saw me.

"Look, Dani! It's Arch's backpack!" Mum had gasped, even though it was totally obvious that's what the something-on-the-doorstep was. I didn't say it, though, cos I had this funny, scratchy, sore sort of feeling in my throat and couldn't speak.

Instead I just read the note taped to the top of the bag. But it was tricky to do, since the funny, scratchy, sore sort of feeling was in my eyes, too, making them water.

And now, Arch's note is tucked in my pocket, all scrunched up. It says...

These guys want to come with you to your new school. See you in the holidays, you big numpty.

Arch

OK, so I have our joint collection of random ex-toys with me, but forty-six random ex-toys don't make up for the fact that I can't mooch around with Arch, hang out with Granny Viv or goof about with Downboy for a whole TERM.

"Ooh! Look, Dani!" says Mum, taking one hand off the steering wheel and wiggling a finger at a stern navy and grey sign by the side of the narrow country road.

My heart sinks into a pit of gloom as soon as I read 'St Grizelda's School for Girls'.

"Doesn't the entrance look grand?" Mum tries to sound perky and positive as she turns the car off the main road and drives through a pair of fancy ornate gates.

I don't answer her – I'm too cross and sad. I just stare at the tangle of trees and shrubs on either side of the lane, with my arms crossed grumpily over my stripy T-shirt.

The only tiny good thing right now is that Mum hasn't been able to get hold of the horrible grey-skirt-and-silly-hat uniform online, so at least I can wear my normal(ish) clothes till someone at the school sorts the problem out.

"Please don't be grouchy, Dani!" Mum tries again. "It's only for three months. And I'm sure there'll be lots of lovely girls to make friends with!"

The thing is, I don't care about making new friends.

I don't need new friends.

I was fine with just one (boy) friend, thank you very much.

And a furry, fuzzy (doggy) buddy, of course.

Not forgetting an OAP (Old Age Pal).

But it doesn't matter how much I sulk.

It didn't matter how much Granny Viv sulked either.

Today I'm being dumped like a bin bag of unwanted bric-a-brac at a charity shop. And in a week's time – after an intensive Antarctica Survival/Penguin Stalking course – Mum sets off on her expedition.

Which leaves the score at:

PENGUINS' BUMS 1   ME 0

Ding-a-ling-a-ling! goes my text alert.

"Who's that?" asks Mum, glancing sideways at me as I scrabble my phone out of my pocket.

"Just Granny Viv..." I mumble, checking the screen.

"Does she want to know what time I'll be

back?" Mum frets. "I did say I'd drop Downboy at hers in plenty of time…"

Mum sounds edgy – Granny Viv's still in a huff and not really talking to her. In fact, it came as a surprise this morning when Granny Viv sniffily announced that since she's "not needed" at home, she's off to look after a poorly friend who lives somewhere unpronounceable in Wales. I'm sure her poorly friend will appreciate that, though I'm not sure that someone who's poorly will appreciate Downboy **"ARF! ARF! ARF!"**ing all over the place…

"She's just wishing me luck," I lie.

My heart is suddenly racing as I read Granny Viv's words.

Dani – I just checked out St Grizelda's NEW website. Your mum must've been looking at a different one, an old one. I just wanted to let you know the school looks TOTALLY

Ploof!

My phone battery chooses THAT exact moment to die. Great. Guess I should've charged it before I left home, like I was supposed to.

"Ooh, Dani, look. Just **LOOK** at this place!" Mum says. I glance up from the irritatingly blank screen. "Isn't it amazing?"

The car crunches on to gravel and a big crumbly old building comes into view.

Amazing? Is Mum crazy?

The building is completely covered in ivy and looks like the sort of place ghosts or murderers live.

Except I don't suppose ghosts or murderers would paint rainbows and bluebirds on their windows.

And hold on. The statue we saw on the website looks as if it's had a makeover. In that photo, snooty St Grizelda wasn't wearing a pair of pink

polka-dot sunglasses and dangling an Elsa-from-*Frozen* lunch box from her hand...

Mum clearly hasn't noticed and is busy figuring out where's best to park.

There're no signs telling visitors to go anywhere in particular so she just aims for the front of the building and pulls up in front of the impressively-huge-but-tatty double front doors.

"Hey, and they've got a dog, Dani!" says Mum, pointing somewhere over to the left of the garden.

At the word 'dog',

Downboy wakes up with a sudden **"Humph?"** while I crane my neck to see what kind it is. But any view of the dog is suddenly obstructed by a bundle of little kids, all mud-streaked and filthy, who've just come shrieking around the corner of the big building and—

THUNK!

Help! Something VERY SCARY has just jumped out of nowhere on to the car bonnet and is growling at us through the windscreen.

"AARGH!" I yell, dropping my mobile on to the floor.

"EEK!" cries Mum, and accidentally presses the horn.

HONKKKKKKKKKK!

"ARF! ARF! ARF!" barks Downboy, clambering over the back seat and up on to my shoulder to get nearer to the Very Scary Thing on the bonnet.

"**RAAAAGHHHHHHH!**" roars the Very Scary Thing.

Is it a ghost? Or a murderer? It looks more like a mutant goblin, with those wild, starey eyes...

I don't know what this weird place is, and I don't know what Granny Viv was going to tell me about in her text. But all I DO know is I have a very BAD funny feeling and want to go home right now – if not sooner... PLEASE!

Chapter 4

Not Pleased to Meet You

And a new head teacher...

A bright, laughing sort of voice cuts through the roaring.

"Off! Get **OFF**, Blossom!"

Wait a sec – the growling, wild-eyed mutant goblin is called "Blossom"?

Whatever it is and whatever it's called, it doesn't get off the bonnet.

I'm just about to tell Mum to start the car and reverse **FAST**, when we hear the laughing person talking again.

"Blossom! I said, **OFF!**"

With a sudden whoosh, Blossom the mutant goblin is lifted into the air by a tanned-looking pair of arms and set down on the ground, where it scrambles to its feet and disappears into the bushes.

"Mum…" I mumble, a tiny bit dazed and confused.

"It's fine, Dani," Mum mumbles back, not

sounding at all sure that everything is fine.

Cos in front of the car stands a grinning woman with two matching mud stripes on each of her cheeks, wearing a Marge Simpson T-shirt, worn jeans and what looks like a crown made of twigs and white plastic spoons.

"**Grrr..**" grumbles Downboy and I completely agree with him.

Mum must've taken a wrong turn. This isn't a school – it's a madhouse. Or a nightmare, maybe?

Quickly I dig my T rex's teeth into my hand to check I'm not asleep and in the middle of some bonkers dream.

Ouch!

OK, so this is real. Really, strangely REAL. (Gulp.)

"Welcome!" the GRINNING woman booms, beckoning us out of the car.

No way.

For a moment no one moves, then the woman steps forwards, opens the driver's side door and ushers Mum to join her.

"Er, hello…" Mum says politely as she climbs out of the car. "Are we in the right place? I'm looking for Ms Murphy, the head teacher of St Grizelda's School?"

"That's me!" beams the woman. "But please call me Lulu. We like to keep things informal here, Mrs Dexter. And this must be Dani!"

Lulu… I repeat in my head, as the scruffy lady with bird's-nest hair smiles in my direction.

On the school website Mum bookmarked there was a welcome message from someone wearing a navy jacket with a stiff dark bob. The name underneath was Ms Louisa Murphy.

I guess if I scrunch up my eyes till everything goes fuzzy, I can see a teeny resemblance.

Yep, it looks like the woman in the plastic-spoon crown is MY NEW HEAD TEACHER.

"Dani!" Mum hisses, motioning me to hurry up.

I warily leave the car, all the time wondering how come Mum disapproves of Granny Viv cos of the way she dresses but is happy for me to be taught by someone wearing plastic cutlery on her head.

But Mum didn't expect this, did she?

What *is* going on?

Was this what Granny Viv was trying to tell me in her text? That my new school is TOTALLY INSANE?

"Oof!" I grunt as Downboy muscles his way out of

the car, too, bashing me aside before he lopes off in search of the other dog to chase.

"Downboy! No – come back here!" Mum calls out as he gallops off round the building, "**ARF! ARF! ARF!**"ing his head off.

"Oh, don't worry. Let him go and explore. I'm sure Twinkle will enjoy a bit of a play," says the head teacher.

Twinkle? Is that the name of the dog Mum saw, or one of the students here? After 'Blossom' the goblin, I wouldn't be surprised…

"Anyway, it's good to meet you, Dani!" booms Lulu, turning to me and holding one hand up.

Uh-oh … she wants me to high-five her?

If I tried to do that to Mr Robinson, my old head teacher, I'd've been in detention every breaktime for a week.

Feeling embarrassed, I give her hand a floppy flap instead of a snappy slap.

"Great," says Lulu, with a grin and a nod like we're now buddies (as if). "And sorry if the Newts startled you."

I have NO idea what she's talking about. And Mum's completely bewildered, too – I can tell by the way her smile has gone all wibbly-wobbly around the edges.

"Blossom and the rest of Newts Class?" Lulu tries to explain, pointing to the rustling shrubs that the mutant goblin – and various 'Newts' – vanished into. "They're our youngest and have huge energy and huge imaginations!"

"Oh, right…" says Mum, glancing sideways at the muddy bare footprints splattered on our car bonnet. "The thing is, there seems to be some kind of a mistake. I thought—"

"You'll meet the Otters and Conkers later," Lulu carries on over Mum's confused mutterings.

Mum and me do synchronized blinking.

"The Otters and Conkers are our Year Four and Five classes," Lulu explains, realizing we're both completely lost.

On the clearly wrong website, I remember noticing that the classes were all named after famous old dead poet blokes, not things from a nature documentary.

"Dani's a Fungus."

"Huh?" I splutter. I'm a WHAT?

"I mean, you're in Fungi Class, Dani," Lulu explains brightly. "Tell you what, while your mum sorts out some boring paperwork, how about you get to know a fellow Fungus?"

Lulu nods over towards a tyre swing I hadn't noticed before, hanging from an old oak tree. Dangling on it, swaying slowly, is a girl who looks like she might be about eleven-ish, same as me.

She has long glossy black hair, hanging straight down to her waist. She is staring at me with narrowed eyes. Lulu might be as bouncy as the Easter bunny, but this girl looks as friendly as a vampire in a really bad mood.

I have a funny feeling we won't be incredibly good friends.

"Wheeeeeeeeep!"

Lulu puts her fingers in her mouth and whistles at the girl loudly, then waves her over.

The girl slowly gets one long leg out from the

tyre swing, followed by the other, and ambles towards me. She's not wearing what I'd've expected – instead of a stiff grey skirt and dumb posh hat, she's in beat-up old flip-flops and dungaree shorts.

"Great stuff! Come on inside, Mrs Dexter," says Lulu. "Swan will keep Dani entertained…"

As Mum follows the head teacher, she gives me a wary look over her shoulder.

I give her a HELP! DON'T LEAVE ME! look back, but she still disappears through the creaking front doors, as if shock has put her into a state of hypnosis.

So, with nervy rumblings in my tummy, I turn round to face my new classmate and mutter a shy "hi".

She doesn't look like she wants to entertain me. In fact, she looks like she might want to sink her fangs into my neck.

"You're Dani Dexter," she says without bothering to give a friendly 'hi' back. She blows a huge pink bubble of gum.

I shrug a yes.

POP! goes the pink bubble, making me jump.

"I'm Swan," she says, sucking the pink back in her mouth with an expert twirl of her tongue.

Swan?! I'm stuck at a school with a goblin called Blossom and a girl called Swan who looks more like Dracula's pretty but equally gloomy daughter?

Then I spot that Swan is staring down at my T rex, whose head I've been twisting without realizing. Aargh! She'll probably think it's just something dumb that I play with.

Quickly I hide my star actor behind my back.

Blow, blow, **POP!**, sluuurppp, goes the pink gum.

"Welcome to St Grizzle's," she says flatly.

"St Grizzle's?" I repeat.

"It's just what everyone round here calls it."
Swan shrugs, ignoring the dinosaur, I'm relieved to
see. "So, I bet you think this place is totally nuts,
don't you?"

"Er, well, it doesn't look much like on the
website," I answer her.

"Hasn't she deleted the old website yet?" Swan
sighs, rolling her eyes and chew-chew-chewing her
gum. "I TOLD her she needed to do that as soon
as the new one went live."

"The head teacher, you mean?" I check with
Swan, wondering what's with the 'old' and 'new'
websites. It must've been what Granny Viv was
trying to tell me about before my phone went
dead...

"Mmm," mutters Swan. "Lulu's so totally useless
sometimes."

I find myself grinning and snort at Swan's

cheeky remark.

Swan glowers at me in return and I stop smiling.

"She's my mum," says Swan, blowing another pink bubble straight at me.

What? Oh, no! This girl is Ms... I mean, Lulu's daughter?

What have I (not quite) said?

Y'know, I think Swan might like me just a LITTLE bit less than stepping in dog-doo. Maybe I should just run and lock myself in the car and refuse to come out.

POP!

I jump again, then wish I could shrivel like Swan's bubblegum in the following awkward silence.

"Hey, you're being watched," Swan says finally. I notice her eyes gazing off into the wooded area to the left of the building.

Spinning round, I scan the trees for something fearsome.

"It's just Zed," Swan says casually. "He's in our class, too."

Ah, I see who she's talking about. This dark-haired, freckly-faced Zed person is hiding behind a silver birch tree. Only he isn't hiding too well. To be fair, it's very hard to hide behind a skinny tree when you're in quite a wide wheelchair.

"He's a **BOY**," I mumble stupidly, wondering how that works at an all-girls school.

"Well spotted," says Swan, giving me a slow handclap. "Still, he gets to be here, cos he's my twin brother and Lulu's the head."

OK, so I have been at St Grizzle's School for Girls, Goblins and Random Boys for about three-and-a-half minutes now and I'm pretty sure I don't want to stay here any longer.

It is completely freaky.

The pupils are stranger than strange.

The head teacher is bananas and I'm not going to—

WHACK!

I'm slammed in the back of the knees with what feels like a plank of wood and I land splat on the gravel. Stars swirl in front of my eyes.

Swan bursts out laughing so hard she nearly chokes on her gum.

From somewhere close by I hear the squeak and thud of a window being opened.

"Everything OK?" Lulu yells. "Oh – I see you've met our school mascot, Dani!"

I lift my head a few centimetres off the gravel.

A hairy face is staring down at me.

When Mum first turned into the driveway,

she'd seen a dog, hadn't she? And for a second –
just before Newts Class went crazy – I'd
wondered what sort it was.

And now I can see quite clearly what kind of
dog it is.

It's the goat kind.

OK, it's **JUST A GOAT**.

"Meh," it bleats bad-
breathed in my face.

"Hey, Dani Dexter,"
giggles Swan,
leering down at
me, along with the
goat and its new,
drooling friend Downboy.
"Meet Twinkle!"

Do I have to...?

Chapter 5

The Tiny, Wriggly, Bit of Hope

And a number of Fungi...

"Don't worry, we'll take good care of her!" Lulu calls out cheerfully from the front steps of the school.

I feel the opposite of cheerful and I'm pretty sure Mum does, too.

As we stand by the car, saying our goodbyes, her hands grip me so tight that I'm worried I'll end up with a fanned pattern of fingerprints on each shoulder.

Meanwhile, I can't help glancing over Mum's shoulder at the thing staring at me from the branches of the nearest tree. It's a grinning goblin, crouched on a branch, all knobbly knees and bared teeth. I don't care if it's really just an eight-year-old girl called Blossom, I'm still scared it's going to eat me.

"I am so, so sorry," Mum says to me, as if there's nothing she can do. But of course there's something she can do. She can put me, my bags

and my dinosaur back in the car.

Right now.

"Hey, Mum – if you grab my suitcase and I grab the backpacks then we can escape before anyone stops us!" I whisper to her.

My heart is heaving with homesickness as I glance from Mum's pretty-but-perplexed face to Downboy's butt (he's licking it right now in the boot of the car).

Cos the thing is, even if St Grizzle's was the Best School in the Entire Galaxy, with classes in Film-making, Paintballing and Dog-snuggling, Compulsory Movie Afternoons (with popcorn), and Help-Yourself Chocolate Fountains in the corridors, I still wouldn't want to stay...

"You know it's just not possible, Dani," Mum says forlornly. "I can't get out of the Antarctica Survival course and I'm already late for the first seminar."

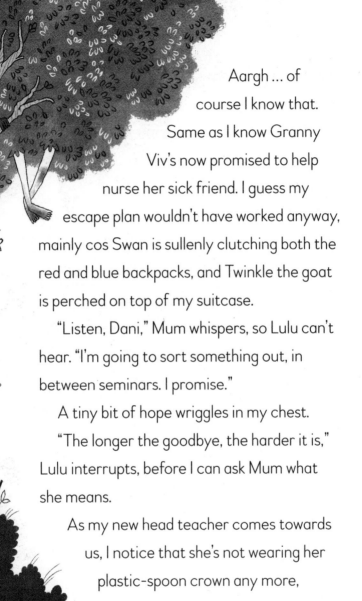

Aargh ... of course I know that. Same as I know Granny Viv's now promised to help nurse her sick friend. I guess my escape plan wouldn't have worked anyway, mainly cos Swan is sullenly clutching both the red and blue backpacks, and Twinkle the goat is perched on top of my suitcase.

"Listen, Dani," Mum whispers, so Lulu can't hear. "I'm going to sort something out, in between seminars. I promise."

A tiny bit of hope wriggles in my chest.

"The longer the goodbye, the harder it is," Lulu interrupts, before I can ask Mum what she means.

As my new head teacher comes towards us, I notice that she's not wearing her plastic-spoon crown any more,

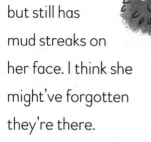

but still has
mud streaks on
her face. I think she
might've forgotten
they're there.

"And – oops!" Lulu adds cheerfully,
glancing at the watch on her wrist. "We're
all late for the next class. Aren't we, guys?"

Lots of voices yelp "yes" in reply, even
though I can't see anyone except Swan
and Blossom the mutant goblin. Oh, and
the silver glint of a wheel as Zed peeks
round the corner of the school building
at me.

The others – whoever they are – are
hidden in the trees and bushes, watching
and listening.

I'm in the middle of a can't-help-
myself shudder when Mum suddenly...

- gives me a quick-but-crushing squeeze of a hug
- plants about fifteen fluttery kisses all over my face
- sobs a hiccuppy "Byeeeee!"
- jumps in the car and speeds off.

So here I am.

All alone.

No family, no friends – just a toy dinosaur to keep me company.

"What am I going to do?" I mumble to my T rex, as I stare down at its tiny head and pointy-teethed grimace.

Only my mumble isn't as quiet as I planned or Lulu has extra-sensitive hearing.

"What ARE you going to do, Dani?" she repeats my words with a smile, putting her hand on my back and gently steering me towards the ivy-tangled school building. "I think the best thing is to follow Swan and she'll give you a tour and show you your dorm. And then you two can come join us in the lesson! OK?"

"OK," I answer in a mouse-sized squeet.

And so I crunch reluctantly across the gravel towards the front doors, where Swan is lifting both my backpacks up on to her shoulders and heading inside.

But as she reaches the doors she pauses. Turning, Swan stares at me with hooded eyes, **POP!**s a pink blob of gum, then shouts, "Oi! Heel!"

What? She's talking to me like I'm a dog now? Well, I...

Oh.

At the "Oi! Heel!" Twinkle leaps off my suitcase with a perky kick of her back legs and trots after Swan as she disappears into the wood-panelled gloom of the entrance hall.

I suppose I'd better do the same. (Without the perky kicks.)

Righting my suitcase, I pull up the extendable handle and rattle and trundle after the girl in the flappy flip-flops and the tippitty-tappetting goat.

"So, the guided tour of St Grizzle's starts here," says Swan, slamming her hand down on a domed silver bell at a hatch in the wall.

DING! DING! DING! DING!

I'm not the only one to have nearly jumped out of their skin.

Beyond the hatch is an office. Inside it, an older teenage boy with spiky black hair yanks a pair of big headphones from his ears and whips his hi-top white trainers off the desk in front of him.

"Hi!" he says, looking like a startled bunny who's just stumbled across a fox. "Yes, please?"

"Toshio, this is the new girl, Dani Dexter," says

Swan, already walking away. "Dani, Toshio is the school receptionist."

"Hi, Dani Dexter," says the older boy in a clipped Japanese-sounding accent, as he gives me a little bow.

"Hi," I reply shyly. Toshio doesn't look much like a school receptionist to me. He looks more like someone who's waiting his turn at the top of a skateboarding ramp.

"Coming?" says Swan, who's waiting for me at the foot of a grand stairwell. By her side, Twinkle is happily chewing at some big leafy plant in a fancy pot.

"If you want to know anything about St Grizzle's –" says Swan as soon as I've caught her up – "then **DON'T** ask Toshio."

"Er, what?" I say, glancing back towards the office window, where Toshio is leaning out, waving, smiling and putting his headphones back on.

"He doesn't speak much English," says Swan, waving back at him. "Lulu sort of rescued him. Same as the goat."

"Huh?" I ask, understanding less the more Swan talks.

"Toshio was on a gap year from his university in Japan, planning on backpacking around the UK. But he got lost straight away. He was looking for Stonehenge when we nearly ran him down in the school minibus last month on our way back from the fish and chip shop in the village."

I don't know what Toshio is studying at university, but I hope it's not geography. Stonehenge is at the opposite side of the country from St Grizzle's.

"He was only meant to stay for tea, and then he was so tired that my mum let him stay the night, which turned into a week," Swan carries on, pausing only for a blow, blow, **POP!**, sluuurppp. "Lulu guessed that Toshio had lost his nerve when it came to travelling, so she did a deal with him. Our old receptionist had just walked out and Lulu offered Toshio the job – temporarily – plus the chance to learn English. He was well chuffed. He doesn't even seem to mind that he's also the cleaner and the gardener, since they left recently, too."

I want to ask why so many staff handed in their notice, but the goat is staring at me, so I ask something different.

"And how did, er, Twinkle get rescued?" I ask, eyeing her warily.

"She was found eating grass on the roundabout of the dual carriageway. Nobody claimed her, so Lulu thought she could live here and be the school mascot," says Swan, as if adopting goats was an everyday sort of thing. "Anyway, all the classrooms are down that way."

With my brain already muddled and befuddled, I glance where Swan's pointing and see an endlessly long corridor.

"And Lulu's office, the dining room, kitchen, Zed's bedroom and stuff are this way," Swan drones on, vaguely pointing at the corridor running in the opposite direction. "OK, follow me..."

Swan begins flip-flopping up the swooping set

of stairs and I scurry after her, badda-banging my suitcase on every step as I go.

That's till my guide – with a silky swish of impossibly straight hair – gives me a glower over her shoulder.

I quickly fumble at the suitcase handle to shorten it so that I can carry the case the rest of the way.

"All the girls' dorms are here," says Swan, resuming the tour as we reach the first-floor landing. "And Miss Amethyst and Mademoiselle Fabienne are in the rooms upstairs."

"Are they two of the teachers?" I ask, thinking fondly of my old teacher, Miss Solomon, even though she's a bit strict and shouty.

"They are ALL of the teachers, along with Lulu," Swan replies. "The rest of the staff left a few weeks ago, when Lulu tweaked the style of the school. So now my mum teaches English and maths and Mademoiselle Fabienne teaches music and art. Miss Amethyst teaches science and drama – usually at the same time."

Swan rolls her eyes and pulls a face.

I gulp.

"Anyway, the Conkers' and Otters' dorms are that way," says Swan. "Newts and Fungi are this direction…"

As she speaks, we pass an old wooden door that's been given a makeover (or been vandalized, as my mum might say). It has handprints all over, in different paint-dripped colours, with a grafitti'd sign that says:

Newts burrow here.
Death to Introoders!!

"This one's ours," says Swan, pausing outside a dark door with a plain, stern, handwritten message pinned to it.

FUNGI DORM
DON'T EVEN THINK ABOUT IT

"It's the perk of being the oldest year group; if you're a Fungus you get one of these," says Swan, holding up a key before twisting it in the clunky lock. "If the dorm was open, the Newts would be in here raiding our stuff and putting our pants on their heads."

"You're joking, right?" I check with her.

"I wish..." drawled Swan, raising her eyebrow.

As I walk in the room I stop still, stunned at the sight of the huge dorm, with its rows and rows and rows of bunk beds.

Urgh.

I think of my small and cosy (and messy) room back home and feel a painful ping of longing in my chest.

"How – how many people actually sleep in here?" I manage to ask, before Twinkle butts me impatiently out of the way so she can go nibble on a pillowcase or two.

"Let's see..." Swan says thoughtfully, quickly counting on her fingers.

While she works out the numbers, I glance

around, blinking as the sun streams
in through the banks of tall windows. All the
endless beds seem neat and tidy except for one
top bunk in the far corner. The duvet there is jade
green and crumpled. A shelf running alongside it
is heaped with books and pretty boxes and bits and
bobs. And on the wall behind the bed head a flurry
of painted birds flutter and fly.

After what feels like a very long time, Swan
lifts her head and gives me the total number of
Fungi I'll be sharing with.

"One."

"One?" I repeat.

"Well, two, now you're here," Swan clarifies.

I blink again, and not just because of the blinding sunshine this time.

"You mean there're only the two of us in our whole year group?" I double-check.

"Two of us girls, plus Zed," says Swan.

"So how many students are at St Grizel—I mean, St Grizzle's altogether?" I ask.

"Altogether?" mutters Swan, beginning to do the counting-on-her-fingers thing again. "I guess there's me and Zed in Fungi; Klara, Yaz, Angel and May-Belle in Conkers; the triplets in Otters and then there are ten Newts. So nineteen, till you turned up."

"But that's less pupils than in the whole of my class at my old school!" I say.

"I suppose the school's pretty small compared

to this time last year," Swan says matter-of-factly. "That's when Lulu first got the job and we moved here. There must have been more than a hundred students back then, I think."

"What happened?" I ask her.

"Well, a couple of months ago, Lulu decided the school needed a change of direction and most of the parents took their kids out faster than Twinkle can eat a flower bed."

POP! goes another pink blob of bubblegum.

It seems like the new-look St Grizzle's is SO unpopular that no one wants to stay, whether they're staff or students...

Well, that's it.

I'm not going to bother unpacking my clothes or random ex-toys... As soon as Mum sorts out something else, I'm GONE.

"Anyway, that's my bed," says Swan, pointing to the top bunk with the halo of birds. "I thought you might like to have the one over there."

Swan has pointed to a bunk that's as far away from hers as it's possible to get. What is her problem with me? Or is she this unfriendly to everyone?

I'm about to follow her and dump my stuff when—

"RAAAAGHHHHHHH!"

roars something horribly close.

"Eeek!" I squeal, dropping my suitcase with a thunk as a mutant goblin flies past the dorm windows, growling.

"Home sweet home," Swan says drily, tossing my backpacks on the bed. "So, ready to go join the class?"

My heart is tap-dancing so fast in my chest that I can't get a word out.

If I could, that word would be a big fat NO.

Chapter 6
A Crazy Kind of Normal

And a mini goth...

Having just seen a flying goblin at the window, I thought the class might be Evil Magic for Junior Witches Etc.

Turns out it was something much more normal.

Well, normal if you go to a school that's run by a crazy person.

"Of course, circus skills are great for confidence-building!" Lulu says cheerfully as she strolls around the back lawn showing me what everyone is doing.

Blossom certainly seems to have a lot of confidence. Right this second she is above our heads on the trapeze rigged up between two trees, very confidently telling her loudly moaning friends down below that they're not getting a turn. Ever.

"Now, over on the far side of the lawn are Klara, Angel and May-Belle, from Conkers class," Lulu chats on, pointing to three girls who are looking at me, whispering and giggling. At the same time, they're dropping the awfully real-looking plates they've been whirling on sticks DANGEROUSLY near each other's toes. "Yaz is in that class, too, but she's probably inside working."

What's 'Yaz' like and why's she working inside? I wonder, as I stare at the plate-spinners. One has very white blond raggedy hair and a Smiley Face T-shirt, one has shiny brown hair and is wearing a gazillion multi-coloured friendship bracelets on both wrists, and the last is in all black – black T-shirt, black leggings, black Converse and a black choker, like a mini goth.

"Oh, and look at THIS," Lulu gasps, and I turn to see three eerily identical girls with tightly braided hair lunging towards us on stilts.

"Well done, triplets!
Great balancing
and— **WHOOPS**!"

Lulu yanks me out
of the way of a bunch
of dirt-streaked, war-
crying Newts who are
cartwheeling themselves
directly at us.

"Close one!" my new
head teacher laughs,
turning to watch as the
Newts spin and roar
onwards past Zed.

And speaking of St Grizzle's One Random Boy, it seems as if being in a wheelchair doesn't exclude him from circus skills class – he's balancing on some kind of extra-wide see-saw, while juggling ... vegetables.

Zed spots me watching, goes so luminously pink that his freckles almost vanish, and – oops! – loses his rhythm. I wince as a carrot and potato land on the grass and a courgette bounces off his head with a soft thunk.

"So, what do you fancy trying, Dani?" Lulu suddenly asks me.

Actually, I fancy trying to call a taxi to take me back to my old school. It's about 11 a.m. now and normally I'd be sitting beside Arch, doing the maths Miss Solomon set us as well as doing our own maths (i.e. counting down the minutes till lunch time when we can plan our next mini-movie).

Maybe it's because I don't answer – or maybe it's because my eyes have gone a bit prickly at the thought of Arch – but Lulu tilts her head and smiles at me.

"Hey, Dani," she says gently. "I know it can be hard to settle in somewhere new."

Somewhere totally new and mad, I think to myself.

"You know, it's even tricky for teachers. You'll meet Mademoiselle Fabienne soon – she only started a few weeks ago and I think she still misses home from time to time."

I think that's supposed to comfort me.

But I'm kind of hoping that right now, Mum is turning the car round on the motorway after realizing...

a) what a terrible mistake she's made, and

b) that I matter LOTS more that stupid penguins' bums.

Fingers crossed, Mum'll collect me before I have a chance to meet Mademoiselle Fabienne or Miss Amethyst, the only other people mad enough to teach at St Grizzle's.

In fact, maybe Mum's already been texting me to say so! I should check my phone... I managed to charge it for a few minutes when I was up in the dorm earlier, while Swan changed her flip-flops for trainers. Annoyingly she was ready before I could see how many bars I had or read the rest of Granny Viv's text.

"Could I go to the loo, please?" I ask Lulu, the excuse suddenly popping into my head.

"Of course!" she replies. "Go through the back door there and..."

I turn away and walk as fast as I can, feeling all eyes on me. All eyes except Swan's; she barely glances my way as she walks barefoot on a tightrope tied between two trees and **POP!**s her bubblegum.

Quickly pushing the back door open I find myself in the panelled hallway and pull my mobile from the back pocket of my jeans.

"Please, please, please...!" I whisper, scanning the screen for signs of a new message from Mum.

Nothing.

So I go to read the full version of Granny Viv's text instead.

It says:

> **Dani – I just checked out St Grizelda's NEW website. Your mum must've been looking at a different one, an old one. I just wanted to let you know the school looks TOTALLY AMAZING** 😈😈😈

Totally amazing?

She looked at a few pics on a website and decided this place is totally AMAZING?

Well, I guess it's easy for HER to say, since SHE doesn't have to stay here in this nutsville place, I think, feeling unexpectedly annoyed by my normally lovely gran.

"No, no, no...!" I suddenly hear an angry voice yelp.

It's coming from a big room to my left, crammed with tables.

I take a step closer to the doorway of what must be the dining room. An older lady is flapping a tea towel and chasing after Twinkle, who appears to be eating an identical tea towel.

"It's bad enough having those GIRLS help themselves to my plates and that BOY take my vegetables without YOU stealing my things!" the lady is shouting, her face beetroot-red with rage. "Oh, NO, you stupid animal. Shoo! You're NOT going in my kitchen!"

As Twinkle skitters off exactly where she's not wanted, the dining room turns empty and quiet.

Almost.

At the scrit-scratch sound of a pencil, I take a step closer and peek my head round the doorway.

A girl is sitting at one of the tables, hard at work. To my surprise, she's dressed in a grey skirt, smart shoes, white shirt and a tie. The uniform of St Grizelda's. Or at least it was, on the old-style website.

I take a step into the room and she glances up at me through dark-rimmed glasses.

"Who are you?" she asks, tugging one side of her neat brown bob behind her ear.

I'm surprised, but I'm not rude. So I shyly introduce myself.

"I'm Dani. But I'm not staying," I tell her.

"Oh, I'm Yaz," replies the girl. "I'm not staying either. My dad's coming for me."

"Really?" I say, edging closer. Great – someone else at this stupid school seems to be normal. We might be the only two.

"Oh, yes," says Yaz, nodding over at the suitcase propped up against the wall, with a straw hat perched on top of it. "In the meantime, I do extra maths during the sillier classes."

Hurray! Till Mum rescues me, maybe this one sane and sensible person could be my friend, even if she's some mad maths fan.

Unless Yaz is leaving any minute, of course…

"When exactly is your dad picking you up?" I ask, feeling a tickle of disappointment in my chest as I glance at her all-packed-and-ready luggage.

"Any time now," she says very definitely. "I emailed him as soon as St Grizelda's went weird, and told him to come and get me."

Er, it doesn't sound as if Yaz's dad is in much of a hurry to rescue his daughter, since St Grizzle's went 'weird' a couple of months ago, according to Swan.

Hmmm ... it seems as if Yaz might not be quite as sane and sensible as I thought.

"So," I say, changing the subject, "who was the lady chasing the goat?"

"That's Mrs Hedges, the cook and housekeeper," says Yaz. "She's from the village and she's worked here forever – but she's not staying either. She hates the changes the head teacher's made. She says it's more like a zoo than a school nowadays and as soon as she finds another job, she's off."

At that moment, my barely charged phone gives a cheerful **Ding-a-ling-a-ling!** as a text pings through.

"I ... I'd better get this," I say hurriedly, turning away.

Is it Mum?

Nope, but it's nearly as good.

> How's it going? Let me know!
> Love Granny Viv xx

And so I give my gran an update.

A one-word update.

> HELP!

Chapter 7

My Cunning Plan

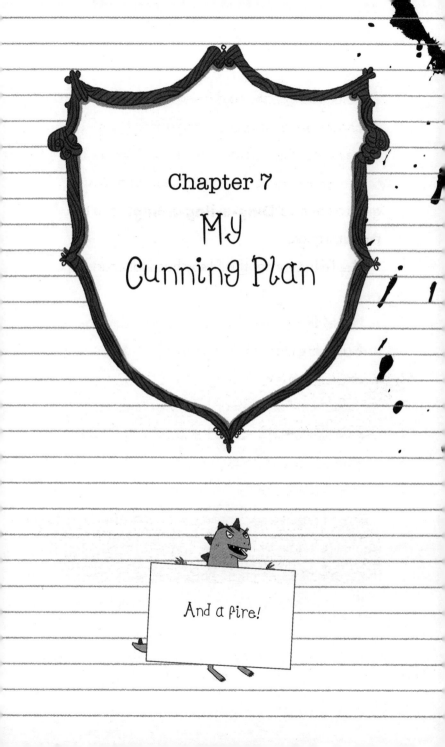

And a fire!

The clock tick-tocks on the empty Fungi dorm wall.

It's three thirty on Monday afternoon and back home – for the first time in forever – Arch will be leaving school and walking home WITHOUT ME.

Hopefully, that won't be the case for too long.

Hopefully Mum will be sorting something out – whatever that something might be – while I'm hiding up here.

OK, so I'm not so much hiding, as pretending to be sick...

This morning, after I'd met Yaz – and her ever-ready suitcase – in the dining room, I realized I needed a Cunning Plan. One that would let me be on my own and away from all the crazy till Mum came back to rescue me.

I was just on my way to reluctantly rejoin the

circus skills class when – **ping!** –  inspiration struck.

So instead of heading for the open back door, I bolted for the girls' loos, where I turned on the hot tap and splashed warm water on my face.

Only then did I return to the garden, where I launched into some **TOTALLY EXCELLENT ACTING**.

"I ... I think I have a fever!" I told Lulu, who immediately got off the unicycle she was riding and felt my clammy forehead.

"Oh dear," she said, frowning in concern.

"AND a tummy ache," I added.

"Oh, that's not good," Lulu said with a shake of her head.

"And I think I might have the collywobbles, too," I said, then wished I hadn't, since I couldn't remember if they were an actual thing or not. Luckily Lulu was completely taken in.

"You DEFINITELY need to get to bed straight away. Here!" she said, and pulled out my Own Personal Dorm Key from the pocket of her jeans.

Yesss!

So, here I am, hours later, not ill at all and very happily on my own.

I have cheered myself up by watching mine and Arch's mini-movies on YouTube a whole bunch of times.

And I've entertained myself by making a new mini-movie, too. In it, the T rex is holding a large tissue in one of his tiny front paws, and staring mournfully out of the Fungi dorm window.

I used a stop-frame animation app on my phone to film him dabbing his eyes, which took a while, cos the tissue kept getting caught in his pointy little teeth and ripping.

After mulling it over, I decided not to do a

voice-over or sound effects for my mini-movie.
I just put up the word 'Homesick...' in this wobbly
sort of font and then let it fade out. It looks pretty
good. Let's see how many views THIS gets on
YouTube...

Click

POST!

I know Arch won't give me a 'like' for a while –
he goes to his trumpet lesson after school on a
Monday. But that's OK; I feel a bit better, a bit
more like me, just by making one of our films.
And it's passed the time while I wait to hear back
from either Mum OR Granny Viv.

"Do you think I should try phoning them?"
I ask my T rex, going over to join him at the
window.

It's only when I'm there that I see something
odd coming from the woods that circle the back
lawn.

Smoke.

SMOKE!

Great grey plumes of it are drifting and noodling above the treetops.

There's a **FIRE?!**

And now that I push open the window, I can hear the strangest jumble of noises; bangs, crashes and high-pitched evil cackling.

And that's not all.

"AHHHH-EEEEE-OOOWWWWWWW!"

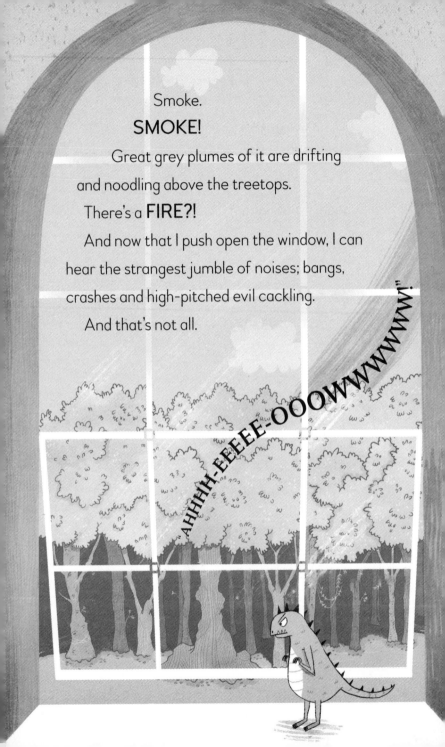

A scream?

Eek! What's going on?

For a second, I'm as still as my T rex, frozen with panic, not sure what to do.

I mean, if I called the Emergency Services, what would I say?

THEM: Emergency Services, how can I help you?

ME: Well, I'd like to report a possible fire-breathing dragon attack...

Instead, armed only with my T rex (kind of useful as a club, I hope), I rush out of the dorm, hurtle downstairs two steps at a time and nearly tumble over Twinkle at the bottom of the staircase, where she's happily tearing off more leaves from the ever-decreasing pot plant.

"Hello!" I call out desperately. "**HELLO?!**"

A whole lot of silence answers me.

Where IS everyone?

Wait – Toshio should be in the school office! He's the receptionist – he'll know what to do...

I hurtle over to the hatch – and see Toshio inside, smiling at his screen, his huge silver headphones blocking out my yelps.

In fact, he's so engrossed in whatever game he's playing on his iPad that a few frantic, arm-waving seconds pass before he even notices me.

"Ah, hi!" he says, finally relieving himself of his gaming stuff and getting up to bow to me. "Yes, please?"

"Something's on fire out there," I say urgently, pointing in the direction of the back door. "And I can hear banging and shouting!"

Toshio tries to follow what I'm saying and keep smiling politely, too.

"Ah, yes. Bang, bang!" Toshio beams and seems to be doing a mime of chopping something.

So what would I say to the Emergency Services now? I think there might be an axe murderer outside, as WELL as a rampaging dragon?

And then I hear the soft tip-tap of footsteps and a "Shh!".

Turning my head sharply, I see the triplets tiptoeing out of the dining room, with bright light from the open back door haloing around their braided hair.

They look like they've been Up To Something. It's not hard to figure that out, since Triplet One is shushing the others, while Triplet Two is shoving something rustly up the T-shirt of Triplet Three...

Oh, but now I think they've somehow sensed that they've been caught in the act and all three turn to stare at me with their almost black eyes in three identical, unsmiling faces.

You know, I feel like someone's signed me up

for a part in a scary, starey horror movie and forgotten to tell me.

Then – whoa! – the triplets do something even more scary that staring. They SMILE!

And each strange smile reveals a chipped front tooth, just like mine...

"Uh, how did you all end up doing that exact same thing?" I ask, crossing the hallway towards them and pointing to my own wonky tooth.

The triplets say nothing. They just each reach up with their index fingers ... and rub a smudge of black off what turns out to be perfectly perfect teeth.

Huh?

They FAKED chipped front teeth ... to mimic me? Why would they do that?

Not that I get a chance to ask. In the blink of an eye – and another rustle – the three girls are gone, disappearing out of the back door and running across the lawn towards the woods...

TRING-A-LING, A-LING-A-LING!

The merry sound of an ice-cream van makes me jump.

It doesn't bother Toshio, though, because he's already sitting down and plugged back into cyberspace.

TRING-A-LING, A-LING-A-LING!

The ice-cream van ringtone – it's Arch

FaceTiming me. I fumble my phone out of my back pocket.

"Hey, Dani!" says my best friend. "Just waiting for my trumpet teacher and thought I'd call you. How's it going?"

Oh, it's so good to see Arch's goofy face and stupid baseball cap.

"Insane!" I hiss.

"Yeah?" Arch replies enthusiastically, thinking I'm being super complimentary about St Grizzle's.

"No – you don't understand," I say, dying for him to get just how nuts this place really is. "Check this out…"

I turn my phone round and point it at the foot of the grand staircase.

"Whoa! The school's got a pet goat?" I hear Arch say. "How cool is that!"

"That's Twinkle, but she's not the main

problem," I say, hurriedly walking past her and heading towards the open back door. "It's the students. And the staff. And the lessons. I mean, get this – you know what our first class was this morning? Circus skills!"

Stepping out on to the sunshiny back lawn, I notice that all the equipment – except for the trapeze swing, now safely tied to a tree – has been packed away somewhere. Or maybe it's been eaten by the rampaging, fire-breathing dragon that's on the loose.

"No way!" I hear Arch gasp. "You didn't tell me they did stuff like that at your new school!"

"That's cos I didn't know they did. And yeah, normally, something like circus skills would be amazing, but that's not the point," I snap, realizing Arch definitely isn't getting it. "Look, there's something seriously weird about this school.

CLANG!

Can you hear that?"

I might be a bit frustrated, but I'm still glad
Arch is here with me. Even if his head is only
about four centimetres wide at the moment, it's
as if he's right by my side. The company of my
best friend is making me braver with every step.

"What am I supposed to be hearing?" he asks.

"Shush and listen," I tell him.

aaaaaah'

BANG! Sure enough, the din and clang of bangs and
crashes is getting louder the closer we get to ...
whatever we're getting close to.

So is the evil laughter, occasional
shrieks and the hiss and crackle of fire.

CLANG!

I stop and hide behind a particularly chunky
oak tree and peer round it, clutching the T rex
close to me with one hand while holding my
phone close to my face with the other. This way,
me and Arch are cheek-to-cheek, and he can see
whatever I'm seeing. kaaaaaaaaaaaaahhhhhhhhhhhhh

BANG!

"What is this, Dani?" I hear him whisper in my ear.

To be honest, I'm not sure, but it's as if we've dived into the pages of a storybook. One of those fairy-tale books that are more full of trolls and warty-faced witches than pretty princesses and happy endings.

There's a huge bonfire in the clearing in front of me. It's so smoky that I can't make out anything properly, apart from a few (hazy) people huddled around it. And behind the bonfire and the huddlers is a tiny wooden cottage – like something out of *Hansel and Gretel* – that appears to be balanced halfway up a tree that's as twisted and gnarled as the one me and Arch are hiding behind. And here's the freakiest thing; small creatures are scrambling over or clinging to the cottage and—

hh!

"AHHHH–EEEEE–OOOWWWWWW!"

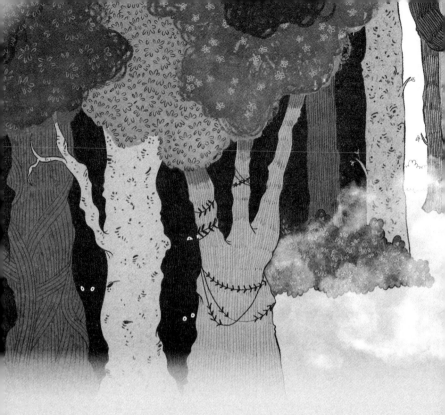

I almost jump out of my skin and drop Arch
with a clatter.

Bizarrely, no one around the campfire seems
that bothered about who's screaming or why,
I realize, as I fall to my knees and frantically
scrabble about in the undergrowth for my phone
and my best friend.

It's then that I know I've been spotted.

Out of nowhere, I'm being pelted with soft somethings that thump and plumpf off my head and arms.

"Arch!" I call out in desperation, at the same time holding up the T rex and using it as a fairly useless shield.

111

"Dani! What's going on?" I hear him call out in concern.

Aha! I spot the phone and snatch Arch up to me, our worried eyes meeting.

"I don't kno— **OOOMMMFF!**"

A squashy something lands directly in my open mouth. All I can hear is Arch's sniggers, and a nearby voice screech…

"BULLSEYE!"

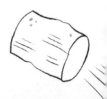

Chapter 8

A
Skippety-hop
of Hope

And a
shopping trip...

No, no, no, NO!

I thought I could outrun them but my hair is caught on something – a branch? – and now they're right behind me and...

My bad dream is suddenly banished by a very loud, very unexpected sound.

"Good morning, good MORNING!"

I sit bolt upright in my bed in the dorm at St Grizzle's as some cheesy, chirpy song blasts me awake.

Only I can't get ALL the way upright because a goat is attached to my left plait.

"Gerroff!" I say, trying to shoo Twinkle away.

Twinkle does NOT gerroff.

"Oi, heel!" my dorm-mate calls over.

Twinkle lets go and trit-trots obediently over to Swan, who is already up, dressed and towel-drying her long hair.

"Good morning, good morning to

YOOOOOOOU!" the loud
voice trills some more.

Where on earth is it coming
from?

"Lulu's idea of a great start to the day,"
says Swan, nodding her head up towards the
speaker above the door, which is belting out a
relentlessly cheerful, old-fashioned musical
number, sung – embarrassingly – by our own
head teacher. "So, did you sleep OK?"

"Mmm…" I mumble, running a hand through
my messy bed-head fringe.

Truth is, I didn't sleep well. I tossed and turned
all night in this strange, echoing room. I must've
fallen asleep at some point, only to end up having
that horrible dream just now, where I was being
chased through the woods by an army of goblins
and a giant fire-breathing penguin.

And another truth is, there were no goblins or

fire-breathing anythings in the woods yesterday. How was I to know that Monday afternoons were always tree-house building class, followed by a barbecue around the campfire?

"You know, you should've stuck around after tea," Swan carries on. "Mademoiselle Fabienne got her guitar out. We all sat in a circle and the little ones sang along. It was kind of fun."

"Mmm…" I mumble again. I wasn't exactly in the mood for fun after being attacked by triplets armed with a bag of stolen marshmallows from the kitchen (see – I knew they were Up To Something!).

And I wasn't in the mood for fun after everyone burst out laughing at the sight of me with a pink marshmallow wedged unexpectedly in my mouth. Including Arch, who got me in such a huff that I switched my phone off.

Of course, Lulu lectured the triplets about…

a) raiding the sweets from the kitchen in the
   first place, and
b) using me as target practice.

She made them say sorry (they didn't LOOK
very sorry, just starey).

Then Zed rolled up beside me and silently held
up a burger, hot off the barbecue, like that would
make me feel better.

But sometimes sorries and snacks just aren't
enough.

Cross and mortified, I told Lulu that I still felt
sickly around the edges and mooched back to the
dorm with my burger. I switched my phone back
on and discovered that MUM HAD TRIED TO
CALL ME while it was off, to let me know that she
had to go to an Extremely Important evening
lecture on How to Lasso a Penguin or something
and wouldn't be able to speak to me till today.

AARGH!

I did manage to talk to Granny Viv for a little bit, which was pretty **AARGH!** too in its own way, since she seemed to be convinced that St Grizzle's sounded fun, fun, fun and not annoying, annoying, annoying. Me and Granny Viv have always been so close, so why can't she get how weird-and-not-wonderful it is for me here? I felt so let down by her that I didn't even get around to asking how her sickly friend was doing in wherever-she-was.

As for Arch, I spent the rest of the evening ignoring his texts and messages, since I was still Extremely Grumpy with him for sniggering at me. He even put a mini-movie up on YouTube of himself with a hand-drawn sign saying "I am an idiot". It made me grin, but I still gave it a thumbs down, just to make him suffer.

"Oh, here we go," Swan says suddenly, staring up at the speaker as the song comes to an end.

"Get ready for the greetings."

I don't know what Swan means exactly but wait for whatever comes next, which could be anything knowing this place.

"Well, hello and happy Tuesday morning to the **NEWTS**!" Lulu's voice booms out, and I hear muffled roars of "Good morning, **LULU**!" coming from the dorm across the hall. One of the roarers will be Blossom, who was to blame for the screams I heard yesterday. Before I left the campfire I saw an older woman all dressed in purple – Miss Amethyst? – yanking a hammer out of Blossom's hand and wrapping large plasters around several of her fingers.

"Good morning, **CONKERS**!"

The four ten-year-olds who make up that class are at the other end of the corridor, so I don't hear their shouts back. I don't suppose semi-sensible Yaz will join in with this goofiness anyway.

"Good morning, **OTTERS**!"

I think of the staring triplets and shudder. I still don't get why they blacked out bits of their teeth. But I bet they pelted me because they knew I knew they were Up To Something – i.e. stealing marshmallows – yesterday.

"Good morning, **FUNGI**… Especially our newest, most fascinating fungus, Dani Dexter!"

Stupidly, at the mention of my name, I blush. (It's especially stupid since I've just been described as a kind of interesting mushroom.)

"And Dani, in addition to this morning's usual lessons, I have a special mission for you. See you at breakfast!"

I look at Swan, hoping she'll give me a clue what Lulu's special mission might be.

Swan just shrugs and – after throwing her towel on an empty bed – heads for the door followed by Twinkle.

Guess I'd better get up and find out for myself, I think, swinging my legs out from under the duvet.

CRUNCH!

My toes were expecting cold lino, but that's not what they got.

"Ow!" I yelp, and my eyes instantly water from the pain of standing on something knobbly and uncomfortable. Blurrily I look down and see a random collection of twigs scattered beside my bottom bunk bed like some 'You're Not Welcome' mat. "What IS this?"

"Gift from Blossom," says Swan.

"Well, it's a pretty dumb gift," I moan, swiping the bits of sticks away with my foot. "I could've got a splinter…"

I hear Swan sigh then close the door behind her with an annoyed-sounding BANG!

Huh? What did I do?

But there's no time to figure it out. I'd better get dressed and see what Special Mission my crazy head teacher has for me…

"Meh!"

I can't believe I'm tying a goat up outside a supermarket, while old ladies and mums and kids give me the strangest looks. I mean, who takes a goat shopping?

Swan and Zed – all the time, apparently. She goes everywhere with them, just like a dog. And since I've got a REAL dog, I've been trusted with wrapping Twinkle's rope-lead around a lamp post, alongside a very wary-looking Jack Russell.

"Yeah, that knot looks strong enough," says Swan as if she's about to award me a Scout badge for Goat-Wrangling.

Beside her, Zed checks the money in a Hello Kitty purse his mum handed him when we left St Grizzle's for our shopping trip.

"Meh!" Twinkle grumbles some more.

"What's up with her?" I ask.

"She can see lunch," says Zed, pointing to buckets of bouquets just inside the entrance to the supermarket.

I stare at Zed in surprise – it's the first time I've heard him speak. He has a shy but sing-songy sort of voice, completely different from his sister's bored growl.

Speaking of bored growls…

"OK, let's do it," says Swan sharply, taking the

shopping list out of her pocket and swooping off towards the store.

THIS is the Special Mission Lulu had for me – and Swan and Zed. According to our head teacher, shopping is a Life Skill, and just as useful as reading and writing and knowing how to make chemicals explode in Science.

Though I think it's more to do with the fact that Mrs Hedges the housekeeper is in a Very Bad Mood with everyone for stealing random plates, vegetables and packets of marshmallows out of her kitchen yesterday.

And so straight after breakfast, armed with wheelie shopping bags, I followed Swan, Zed and Twinkle out of the school's shabby-but-not-chic double front doors. We rumbled past the statue of St Grizzle – today wearing Lulu's plastic-spoon crown on her head plus a pair of yellow rubber gloves – and set off down the driveway to the lane that would take us to the village.

There wasn't much talking on the way, since we had to walk in single file, keeping an eye out for traffic. Swan flip-flopped at the front, with her own wheelie bag and Twinkle on a lead, with Zed pushing himself along behind, shopping bag dangling from the handles of his chair, and me trundling reluctantly in the rear.

And now we're just about to go into the supermarket on the busy, bustly High Street of the village when I can't help noticing that we're being stared at by passing schoolkids, all dressed in matching black trousers and green sweatshirts.

"Hold your noses!" shouts a tall boy with a floppy blond quiff. "It's some smelly Grizzlers!"

The boy has that look that all meanies do, a smile that has not one speck of niceness to it.

I feel my cheeks instantly pink up.

Swan doesn't go pink. She stays silent and super-cool, gives the boy with the quiff a Fierce Death Glare and blows a spectacularly big bubblegum bubble.

POP!

The boy looks like he's about to say something, then can't think of anything clever, so just sneers instead.

Swan spins away from him, her black hair

flapping like a victory flag, and right on cue the supermarket doors glide open for her.

Following her in, I sneak a sideways glance at Zed and see he's giving me one back – along with a small, shy smile. I realize it's the first time I've seen him smile. I manage a shy smile back.

"Wow, she is seriously fierce," I mutter as I wrestle a trolley free from a parked row and watch Swan sauntering off along the vegetable aisle.

"Tell me about it," Zed replies, giving me something that's pretty close to a grin.

"Is she always like that?" I whisper as we wheel after his sister.

"Pretty much." Zed shrugs. "Though she's more ratty than usual at the moment..."

Zed suddenly looks thoughtful, but I don't feel I know him well enough to ask what he's thinking OR why Swan's quite so grumpy. Especially now we're catching up to her.

"Who was that boy and his mates?" I ask as carrots and courgettes land thump-thump in the trolley, casually chucked there by Swan.

"The one doing the talking was Spencer," says Zed.

"Him and his friends go to the village school and they think everyone at St Grizzle's is a rival. Like we actually care that much," Swan drawls. "And Spencer's been making the 'smelly' remarks ever since Lulu ditched our uniform and we got Twinkle. He thinks he's hilarious."

"Which he's not," says Zed, crinkling his freckly nose.

"Tell you what WAS funny," Swan says, turning to her brother. "When you accidentally on purpose ran over his toes last week in the crisp aisle!"

Certain things are catching, aren't they? Like colds, yawns and laughter.

So when Swan and Zed start sniggering, I find myself grinning, too. It feels good. I don't think I've felt happy like this since just before Mum told me about the Antarctic Expedition and everything in my world went twisty and odd.

And once the laughing and the grinning ebbs away, I think of a question I'd like to know the answer to.

"Did you guys like the school better the way it

was, or the way it is now?" I ask.

"Now, of course," says Swan, looking at me as though I'm a nitwit. "It's a LOT more fun. Not that it's going to be for very much longer..."

"What do you mean?" I ask as Swan swans off, grabbing shopping here, there and everywhere and me and the trolley struggle to keep up.

"Our mum thought everyone would like a school that's more fun," Zed answers instead, zooming along by my side. "Turns out they don't."

"Which is why most of the parents pulled their kids out," Swan says over her shoulder as she checks the price on a mega-bag of marshmallows. "And if kids KEEP leaving, the school won't be able to afford to stay open."

At that last remark, a thought zaps into my head. THIS is the reason Swan is extra-ratty at the moment – she's worried!

For a second, I feel a teeny flicker of pity for

her – but that quickly vanishes when I realize that I have a little skippetty-hop of hope in my heart.

Cos if St Grizzle's closes down soon, I'll HAVE to go home! Whether that means sleeping in a cupboard at Granny Viv's, or me and Granny Viv and Downboy squatting in the building site at our house, or maybe even Mum ditching the penguins and Antarctica for ME!

Swan is too busy zipping through the shopping list to see the gladness lighting up my face – but Zed does.

"You don't like it at St Grizzle's, do you?" he asks, with a look on his face like a puppy left out in the rain.

"It's not that," I say, feeling myself blush again. "It's just—"

"Just that you aren't giving it a chance, Dani," Swan says icily, grabbing the trolley from me and pushing it to the nearest till. "It's OK, you're not the only one. I just feel sorry for the younger kids. It's not great for them to see people turning up their noses at the students and the school."

I'm turning super-pink now. Is that what they think I'm doing? I'm not 'turning up my nose' at the Otters and Newts and everyone. THEY'RE the ones giving ME a hard time, mimicking the way I look and pelting me with sweets and cartwheeling themselves at me menacingly...

"That's not fair," I say, feeling an achy twang in my chest at being misunderstood.

"Well," says Swan, beginning to pack the shopping into her wheelie bag as soon as it's swiped, "you weren't exactly grateful for Blossom's gift this morning, were you?"

"The sticks?" I say in surprise as Swan shoves a bag of potatoes into my arms.

"She'd laid them out while you were still

sleeping," says Swan. "They spelled out, 'Hello, Dani Dexter!' Well, actually, it said 'Hello, Dani Dexterer!' – she hasn't quite got your name right yet. But whatever, it was meant to be a nice surprise."

Oh … that mess was a message? For me?

I have a horrible feeling that I might've got things a little bit wrong.

But I'm not the only one.

"Stop! NO!" comes a shout from nearby. "Leave those flowers alone!"

Uh-oh. Speaking of sticks, Twinkle has somehow got herself free, trotted into the supermarket and is speedily turning a bouquet of roses into a bunch of thorny twigs.

As Swan and Zed hurtle over to grab her, I do the obvious thing – snatch my phone from my pocket and take a photo.

'My start to the school day,' I text to Arch,

Granny Viv, and – most importantly – Mum.

If the sight of a goat running up the cheese aisle with a red rose in its mouth doesn't get Mum driving here to rescue me, then I'm DOOMED...

Chapter 9
The Egg Box of Gloom

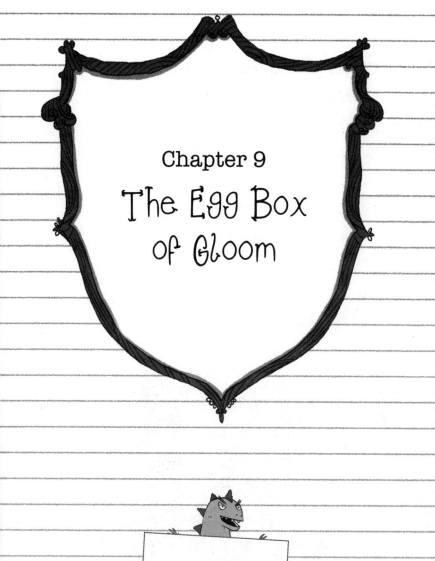

And a most
peculiar feeling...

Think of a recycling bin.

Imagine it upturned on to a table.

Welcome to my first proper lesson of the day, art class, with the whole school – all twenty of us.

Now think of a bum.

Imagine it vibrating.

That'll be my phone, turned to silent mode in my jeans' pocket.

I slip it out and sneak a look at the screen to see who's texting.

Granny Viv!

She's got back to my message about Twinkle's supermarket spree.

But my smile of happiness fades when I see her reply.

I wanted her to say something like...

'My goodness, that's ridiculous, my darling Dani! I'll ditch my sick friend and come get you immediately, if not sooner!'

Instead, her message just reads...

HA HA HA HA HA HA HA HA HA HA HA!
So funny! 😆 😆 😆

Sighing, I put the phone down on the table in front of me and flick to YouTube, and me and Arch's mini-movies. But not even the sight of all the Beanie Boos as Hobbits (with dusters for cloaks) can cheer me up.

I'm not stressing about being caught on my phone, by the way. Mademoiselle Fabienne, the art teacher, is too busy to notice. She's perched on her desk, strumming a guitar and singing something very sad-sounding in French. I'm no expert, but it doesn't seem much like it's got anything to do with art, or today's subject that's flashed up on the whiteboard: 'Make What You Feel Inside'.

Around me, the others are taking their time, constructing teetering, blobby or complicated-looking things out of milk cartons, cereal boxes, cardboard tubes and assorted bobbins, all held together with lashings of parcel tape.

That's everyone apart from the triplets, who are silently and happily gluing their fingers together.

Oh, and Yaz. She's sitting beside me with her open maths book, doing something technical with fractions.

And me? I've finished my work already. As soon as I sat down I grabbed an egg box and painted it turquoise. Rubbish and blue, that's how I feel. I should call it The Egg Box of Gloom...

I flick to another mini-movie (Elmer as Batman, with a costume made from scraps of bin bag), but a movement outside the window catches my eye. Out on the back lawn, a frowny Mrs Hedges is attempting to peg some flapping bed sheets to the washing line while at the same time trying to stop Twinkle from butting her in the bottom.

As I idly watch the mayhem, I think back to this morning and feel relieved that Swan and Zed didn't think I was to blame for Twinkle's escape. I mean, I may not be an expert at goat knots, but I was pretty sure I'd tied her rope-lead up nice and tight to the lamp post outside the supermarket. In fact, Swan and Zed seemed pretty positive that Spencer from the village school had something to do with it...

I'm just remembering Spencer's meanie sneer when I hear a small sniffling sort of sound.

I turn my gaze away from the goat-and-grumpy-lady battle going on outside and look around the room for the source of the sniffle.

No one else seems to notice it – they're too wrapped up in describing their feelings with junk.

Uh-oh … the sniffler – it's Mademoiselle Fabienne!

Is she – is she crying a little bit?

She's stopped strumming mid-tune, her head drooped, her long fair hair dangling over her guitar. Wait – didn't Lulu say she was newish and homesick? Has she been making sad music, to show what's inside?

That makes me feel all kerfuffled.

Cos if someone in class is upset, you put up your hand and tell the teacher.

But if your teacher is upset, who do you tell?

I'm pretty sure a teacher wouldn't want all their pupils to see them feeling wibbly.

So I should DO something... I just don't know what.

And then I have an idea. Scrabbling around in my hoodie pocket, I find a clean tissue. I scribble something on it in black felt pen, then stand up, grabbing a nearby pencil and sharpener.

The bin is by Mademoiselle Fabienne's desk. I walk over, and quick-as-I-can pass the tissue to the sniffly teacher, then pretend to sharpen the already-sharp pencil.

Miss Fabienne looks down at the tissue in her hand. I hope she knows enough English to understand what I've written.

I feel homesick too...

Mademoiselle Fabienne looks up at me with tear-pooled eyes, gives me a watery smile, then blows her nose loudly and gratefully on the tissue, leaving only the tiniest transfer of black felt pen on her left nostril.

Not wanting to draw attention to our teacher, I pootle back to my seat, feeling all glowy inside. And then I panic a little, when I see that my phone is NOT where I left it.

"You did this?" whispers Yaz, lifting a page of her maths book to reveal my mobile, showing a T rex in a red cardboard phone box, miming along to Adele's 'Hello'.

She must know I did, since 'A Dani Dexter & Arch Adams Film' is the strapline underneath.

"Yes, me and my best friend make … made them all the time," I say, correcting myself and feeling more like my painted egg box than ever.

"You have more? Could you show me them later?" Yaz asks, her dark eyes bright and shiny and excited with something other than maths.

Ooh, and I've just had the most peculiar feeling.

Deep inside, hidden among the horrible homesickness and the big blue gloom, is a tiny sliver of sunshiny yellow.

Hello happiness... I've missed you!

It's nice – just me and Yaz are in Fungi dorm right now, since Swan ambled off into the garden with the others after tea.

What's nicer still is that the yellow smidge of happiness keeps glowing and growing as I set out all forty-six ex-toys in rows along the dorm windowsills.

At first Yaz is a bit bamboozled at the sight of them, but when I hold up my phone and show her the various ex-toys' acting skills, she's well impressed.

"Could you show me how to do films like yours?" Yaz asks, staring starstruck at the unicorn after seeing it prance along to 'Let It Go'. "I'd love to make some myself, just as soon as I get back home and dig my old toys out of the attic."

"You don't have to use ex-toys," I tell her. "You could just get a packet of googly eyes from a craft

shop and stick them on anything – fruit, spoons, acorns – and turn them into characters!"

"Ha!" laughs Yaz. "That would be fun. But my dad will be here ANY time to get me, so I'll probably wait till then."

I get the feeling that it's just Yaz and her dad, same as it's just me and Mum.

"So, um, what does your dad do?" I ask, staring at Yaz's neat knot in her tie and wondering why her father hasn't managed to rescue her from St Grizzle's quite yet.

"He's a diplomat, so he travels a lot for work," Yaz answers as she examines some more of my characters.

"Sounds important," I say, not really knowing what a diplomat does exactly. "My mum's a zoologist. She's going to be travelling, too – to Antarctica to study penguins for a really important project."

"No way! That is SO cool!" says Yaz, sounding impressed.

The yellow glow inside me grows even more and suddenly I'm kind of impressed by Mum, too...

CLUNK!

The dorm door is flung open and Swan sticks her head round it.

"Hey! We're going to have another campfire tonight. Coming?" she asks.

The yellow glow expands.

You know, I think I'd like to.

Today started on the wobbly side, but it's got better. After art we had lessons that were almost normal (though back at my old school we weren't made to do star-jumps between maths and English sessions to "shake free" our energy). Even if Mrs Hedges served lunch and tea with a sour face, the food was pretty yummy. And showing off what I do best (directing my mini-movies) to my new friend Yaz has made me feel less all-alone. So maybe it would be kind of fun to hang out by the campfire, since I'm stuck here for another night at least.

I'm about to say so when Yaz jumps in.

"Nope, we're all right as we are, aren't we, Dani?" Yaz says confidently.

"Suit yourself," Swan says with a couldn't-care-less shrug.

As the door thunks closed behind her, I look over the heads of my ex-toys and gaze at the scene on the back lawn down below.

Zed is being pushed across the grass by blond, tangled-haired Klara, who's panting and laughingly complaining about how hard it is. That's cos Blossom is standing barefoot on the armrests of the wheelchair, hands outstretched, yelling "I'm King of the World!" as Zed grips her round the waist to stop her from falling off.

"Idiots," says Yaz, coming to gaze out of the window, too.

"Definitely," I hear myself agreeing with her.

But as Klara, Zed and Blossom disappear into the woods, I feel my sunshiny glow fade and long blue shadows sneak back in.

Chapter 10

Newts, Goblins, Meerkats, Whatever

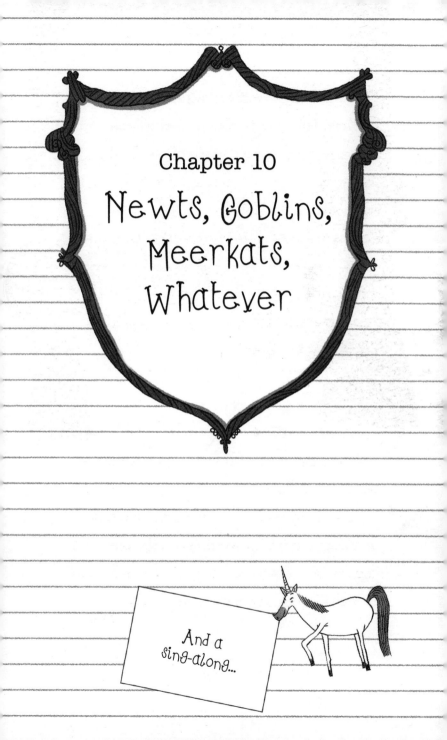

And a sing-along...

First lesson on a Wednesday morning, you'd normally find me partnering up with Arch in PE, in the gym that always smells of feet.

But that was at my old school and nothing is normal at St Grizzle's.

This Wednesday, my first class of the morning is a whole school science lesson. There's classical music playing softly in the background, the Newts have all come in wearing their clothes back to front, a goat is snoring under the teacher's desk and someone has just snuck up behind me in a wheelchair.

"**Fnnnntttt!**"

Zed's rubber tyres were completely silent on the lino just now, unlike his snigger.

"That is SO funny," he says, grinning at the image on my screen, the one I was just showing Yaz.

"Shh!" I whisper, checking that our teacher

hasn't heard him. I don't want to get into trouble for being on my phone. Luckily Miss Amethyst's too busy trying to get the giggling Newts to settle down, which is a bit like trying to herd skittering kittens.

So I sneak a look back at my screen again and Zed's right – it is funny. It's a selfie of Arch with the title 'What class is like without you'. It's a photo of him snoozing at his desk.

And there's another funny something on my phone this morning. I missed a call from Granny Viv when I was at breakfast and, listening back to the message, all I could make out was a whole bunch of snuffling and schlurping noises. Then Granny Viv bursts in and says, "That's just Downboy saying hello!"

Less funny and more important was the message from Mum, apologizing for the game of Missed-Call Ping-Pong we've been playing the last couple of days. Of course I'm still cross with her for sending me here, but it has been nice to hear her voice, and her Penguin conference stories. In today's message, she said she's pretty sure she's got something sorted at last about school and that she can't wait to tell me about it!

I showed Yaz the message on the way to class. She reckons Mum and Gran will have made up, and that Gran's going to come back from Wales, and that I'll go and live with her – which would be great, even if it does mean sleeping on her tiny two-seater sofa with my knees up to my chin every night. Yaz also reckons that Mum will be here on Saturday morning, as soon as her conference is finished, and that I'll be packing the ex-toys in the car and waving goodbye to all the girls and goblins of St Grizzle's – and Zed the random boy, of course.

In the meantime, I just need to be patient and—

"Teach!"

A vision in layers of purple slams her hands down in front of me on the desk.

I blink up at Miss Amethyst, whose puffs of grey hair are tinged with mauve.

"Sorry?" I say in my mouse-squeet.

"As the eldest in the school, I expect the Fungi to help teach the younger children from time to time. It's a useful Life Skill, you know! So, are you up for it, Dani?"

"I don't think I—"

"Of course you can," Miss Amethyst says confidently, rolling up the sleeves of her purple cardie. "Here are some fun worksheets on the Food Chain. It's on the whiteboard, too. Just talk the Newts through it and help them with the questions. Now the rest of us are heading outdoors, for a hands-on biology session!"

And with that, Miss Amethyst strolls over to the classroom door and holds it open, ushering Swan, Zed, the Conkers and Otters out into the corridor.

The Newts, who were madly chitter-chattering and scampering around the desks till a second ago, are now staring at me, stock-still.

"But I don't know what I'm doing and—"

"Nonsense, Dani. You'll rise to the challenge, I'm sure!" booms Miss Amethyst. "Just make sure you put your mobile away first, though, dear."

The sight of her raised eyebrows as she exits

154

the room make me blush. So being left with the Newts is really a punishment for being on my phone, isn't it?

For a second, the silence presses heavily as I stare at the Newts and the Newts stare at me.

It's broken by Blossom.

"Would you like to see me tap-dance, Dani Dexterer?" she says, and begins tippitty-tappetting noisily and out of time.

The other Newts start giggling, whooping and clapping along, also out of time.

Then there's even MORE tippitty-tappetting as Blossom accidentally dances on to Twinkle's tail, making her wake up, clatter upright and "MEH!" loudly in annoyance.

"Stop!" I shout as loudly as I can and hurry over to the front of the room, plonking myself on to Miss Amethyst's chair. "What I'd like you all to do is sit down."

I gaze from the worksheets to the whiteboard – they don't match up. Help!

"I said **SIT DOWN**!" I call out, above all the shrieking and giggling.

In a panic, I press arrows back and forth on the computer keyboard. Page after colourful page on science topics pops up, but not one of them is about Food Chains. Help, help, HELP!

"We ARE sitting down!" I hear Blossom say.

I give a quick glance up from the computer and see ... an empty classroom.

Then the tops of a few heads give the joke away – the Newts are all hunched cross-legged on the floor between the tables.

This is **AWFUL**.

What am I going to do with these daft little girls till Miss Amethyst gets back?

I didn't know it was possible to be burning hot and freezing cold at the same time but my insides suddenly feel exactly like boiled ice cream.

I'd give anything to be hanging out with Arch right now in the whiffy gym instead of being trapped here with Blossom and her gang of goblins...

Then a memory pings into my head, of me and Arch doing some science project round at his one day. Mucking about online and only half-heartedly doing our research, we found the funniest video. It was called 'The Periodic Table Song' and the words were just the names of ALL the gases and chemicals there are, sung over super-fast, old-time waltzy backing music. Ignoring our project, me and Arch spent the whole afternoon bouncing around his bedroom and learning the song – and all one-hundred-and-something elements in the Periodic Table.

Ka-boom!

That's it! With my fingers flying on the computer keyboard, I find what I'm looking for and press the play arrow.

"THERE'S HYDROGEN AND HELIUM..."

As soon as the goofy song and video starts up, girls pop up from between the desks like inquisitive little meerkats.

Yesss!

I've got them.

For the whole of the video clip, ten heads nod, ten pairs of eyes sparkle, ten dirty faces beam.

Watching them, part of me is hopeful that I can turn this gaggle of Newts/goblins/meerkats/whatever into a Chemistry Choir that'll impress both Miss Amethyst and the rest of the school – all nine of them.

The other part of me suspects they'll just blow raspberries and run shrieking and roaring out of the classroom door in their back-to-front outfits, leaving me with:

a) Twinkle, and

b) my trainer laces unexpectedly tied together.

But I have to try, right?

"OK," I say, as the song ends. "Are we all ready to sing along?"

"Yeah!" cry the Newts.

"Meh!" bleats Twinkle.

Wish me luck, I think to myself...

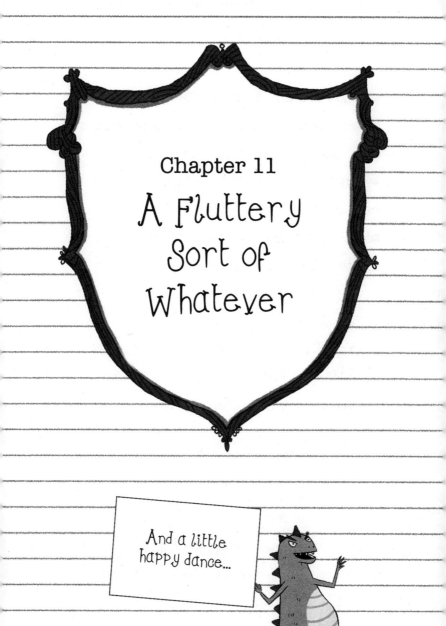

Chapter 11
A Fluttery Sort of Whatever

And a little happy dance...

Who knew washing-up is another Life Skill?

Lulu certainly thinks so, which is why each of the classes at St Grizzle's take their turn in the kitchen, cleaning the cups and plates, pots and pans after tea. (Yaz also thinks it's because our head teacher can't afford to hire any more staff till there are a lot more pupils. Which means it's never going to happen, obvz.)

I don't mind washing-up, though – I do it all the time at home with Mum. We chit-chat while the radio babbles away in the background, and everything's sparkling and clean before we know it.

It's kind of like that this Wednesday evening in the big school kitchen, only instead of Mum, I'm passing warm soapy dishes to Swan. She in turn piles the dried washing-up on to the waiting lap of Zed, who then zooms and puts it all away on shelves and in cupboards.

"We'd normally have music on," says Swan, "but that needs repairing…"

I look over where she's nodding and see a silver radio on the windowsill. A white lead dangles down … then stops a few centimetres above where a plug must have been.

I'm about to ask what happened to the missing piece of cable when I glance out of the kitchen window and see the probable culprit.

In the evening sun-filled garden, I see Yaz sitting at a picnic bench, doing a maths test paper for fun, completely unaware that Twinkle has ambled off with her fluffy pencil case for pudding.

Anyway, me, Swan and Zed wouldn't be able to hear much of what was on the radio even if it was working. The Newts are all roosting in the trees outside, dirt-streaked legs dangling from branches as they yell 'The Periodic Table Song' over and over and over again.

(I may regret teaching them that,
no matter HOW impressed Miss Amethyst
was with the Chemistry Choir.)

"Right, all done," says Swan, drying off the
last glass and passing it to Zed. "Coming to the
campfire tonight, Dani?"

I HAD planned on doing what I've been doing the last couple of evenings – moping, messaging and watching my mini-movies for the twelfty-trillionth time, maybe with Yaz again, if she's up for it.

"Please come, Dani!" said Zed, giving me his freckly nosed, pleading-puppy look.

The thing is, there's no point in me hanging out with everyone. I can't go starting to be friends with all these weird people when I'm going to be leaving super-soon, can I?

But then I look back out into the garden and sigh...

Out there, everything is bathed in warm orange light, the butterflies are doing a little happy dance from shrub to shrub and wood smoke is curling and swirling above the treetops.

Gazing at all that I realize the last thing I want

is to be cooped up in the dorm again.

I want to feel cool grass between my toes, have a closer look at the tree house that's being built and hopefully toast marshmallows by the fire (instead of having them fired AT me).

It'll be OK to have a little fun. It doesn't mean I like it here at St Grizzle's.

"Yeah, why not," I say, pulling the plug out of the sink and letting the soapy water gurgle away.

"Cool!" says Swan, looking pleasantly surprised. "I'll just go get my spray paint from the dorm..."

"She'll get her what?" I ask Zed, not sure I heard right.

"Wait and see," he grins back.

A fluttery sort of uh-oh rumbles in my tummy...

The fluttery uh-oh carries right on rumbling.

Cos I'm seeing all right, and I don't much like what I'm seeing.

Swan has climbed up the ladder to the wonky-but-cute, half-built tree house and is shaking a can of black spray paint, about to graffiti school property.

"You're not seriously going to do that, are you?" I call up to Swan.

She turns and possibly grins at me (it's hard to tell, she's wearing a white mask over her nose and mouth).

"Shouldn't we try to stop her?" I ask Zed, aware that as the oldest in school, we should maybe be setting a good example to the younger ones.

I glance around at Toshio, too – he's currently on campfire duty as a 'responsible' adult – but all he does is smile and give me a thumbs up, while nodding his head to the music blasting in his headphones.

Zed's not any more reassuring. All he does is tap the side of his freckly nose and wobble his eyebrows teasingly.

I feel my heart pitter-pattering... I know Lulu runs this school a little differently. A little looser. A little arty-fartier. But surely even SHE is bound to be as angry as the most ordinary, old-fashioned head teacher if she sees some ugly TAG spray-painted over something the students have been working on so hard.

"Please, Swan!" I begin to beg her. "Don't do—"

But with a fizz and a hiss she does.

And what she does is long arcs of black, going this way and that.

One arc swooping down turns into a body. Two arcs swooping up become wings in flight. With smaller, quicker bursts, a head and beak take shape.

When she finally finishes and jumps back down to earth to join us, me, Zed and Toshio are transfixed by the sight of the huge and perfect crow, now flying by the side of the crooked tree-house door.

"How do you do that?" I ask her in awe.

"Just practise with lots of smaller drawings first," she says with a pleased smile.

I think of the colourful birdie flock above her bed and realize Swan must've painted those herself. Wow.

"I've got a whole folder of bird drawings under my bunk," she carries on. "And that's why it's good to be able to lock the door to the dorm. It doesn't just stop the Newts invading; it stops goats from eating your artwork."

Then a totally unexpected thing happens – we both snigger at the same time.

And here's the MOST unexpected part. With those matching sniggers, it's like something's twanged and loosened and relaxed between us. It's almost – and this is freaky – as if we were friends.

I glance round to see if Zed's giggling, too.

Oh. He's not. In fact, he looks worried.

"Er ... Swan, are you sure you locked the door to the dorm before you left?" he asks his sister.

"Course I'm sure I—"

When Swan stops mid-sentence and looks behind me, I know something has gone wrong. BADLY wrong. **NOISILY** wrong.

I turn and see Twinkle – happily crunching on a T rex.

MY STAR ACTOR, T REX!

I lunge at Twinkle and she leaps delicately sideways.

I lunge again and she leaps the other way, with a perky kick of her back legs.

I lunge one more time and she boings neatly out of my grasp.

"Please, tell her to 'heel'!" I shout over at Swan as I chase the goat and the half-chewed dinosaur around the campfire.

Swan – like Zed and Toshio – is struggling to breathe she's laughing so hysterically, which means she's no help at all.

You know, I have SO had enough of St Grizzle's School for Girls, Goats and Random Boys.

GET ME OUT OF HERE!

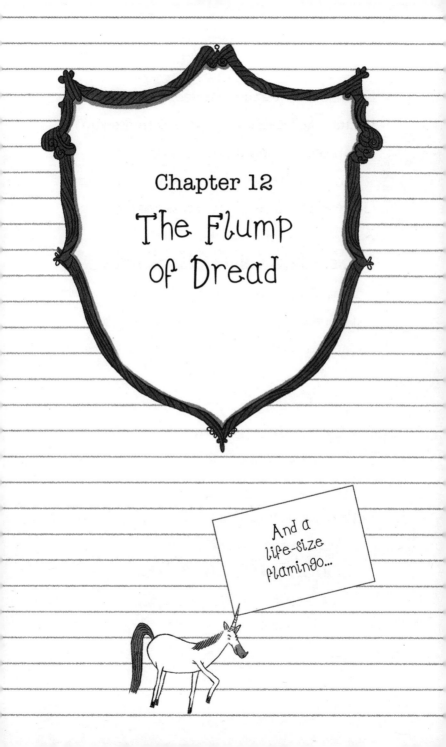

Chapter 12

The Flump
of Dread

And a
life-size
flamingo...

Lulu might've wished us a "Happy Thursday!" over the tannoy this morning, but the atmosphere in the Fungi dorm was pretty gloomy.

"Look, I said I was sorry," Swan announced, standing over my bed, a towel draped over her arm and a toothbrush in her hand.

But I was too upset to answer her back. Swan didn't understand – she thought my dinosaur was just a dumb toy, not something precious that reminded me of Arch and home and everything I missed.

Instead, I rolled over and buried myself under the duvet, so that any more of Swan's empty words and fed-up-with-me sighs were just muffled nothings.

But now, an hour later and in Lulu's office, I heard a different sort of noise.

SQUOOOFFFLE-pffffffffffff...

The last time I was in a head teacher's office

was at my old school, when Mr Robinson wanted to praise me for my 100 per cent attendance. It felt horribly awkward sitting down on his creaky plastic visitor's chair.

But sitting down in Lulu's office is a whole new level of awkward. I lowered myself into the beanbag as carefully as I could just now, but it still made that embarrassing soft'n'squelchy noise.

"Would you like a meringue? The triplets made them," says Lulu, pointing to a plate on her desk that's piled high with wonky blobs that look like slightly singed, melted lumps of foam. (When I saw Mr Robinson he offered me a chewy toffee that glued my teeth together so all I could dribble was "Ang-ooo" when he gave me my attendance certificate.)

"No, thank you," I say, nice and clearly.

I'm not just being non-greedy. Yesterday afternoon, I passed the kitchen when Otters class

were having their cookery lesson with grumpy
Mrs Hedges and saw...

- one of the triplets drop the whole tray of
  meringues on the floor
- another triplet gather them all up
- the third triplet dust floor fluff off the
  meringues with the corner of the top she'd
  been wearing for the last three days.

"Anyway, you must be wondering why I've
asked you here, Dani," says Lulu as she carries on
watering the jungle of plants in the room.

Mr Robinson just had a faded posy of fabric
flowers on his desk. He also had a framed picture
of his daughter. Behind Lulu's desk is an entire
wall that's spray-painted with rainbow-beaked
toucans and a life-size flamingo, courtesy of
HER daughter.

"I suppose ... a little bit," I say.

A LOT, actually.

To be specific, all through breakfast I'd wondered two things...

1) where Swan was (she hadn't come down from the dorm), and

2) why Lulu had boomed though the tannoy that she needed to see me once I'd finished eating.

Yaz had her theories.

"Maybe Swan's too embarrassed to face you after what happened with your dino-thingy," she'd whispered to me in the dining hall as I picked at my beans on toast. "And hey, maybe Lulu's heard from your mum!"

I was so excited at the idea of Mum calling – and telling Lulu when she was picking me up – that I couldn't eat a bean more.

Instead I'd hurried along to Lulu's office straight away, dodging a lobbed cabbage as a couple of Newts played a game of ten-pin bowling in the corridor.

And so here I am – not so much perched on the edge of my seat as squiggled in the middle – waiting to find out when I need to get my bags packed and ready...

"Well, I just wanted to say that it's been really terrific having you here at St Grizzle's this week, Dani!" Lulu says brightly.

And...?

There's got to be an 'And...', hasn't there? And we'll miss you when your mother comes for you...? THAT sort of 'And...' is what I want to hear next.

"And I've been hearing such lovely things about you," Lulu carries on. "You've really made quite an impression on everyone."

OK, so not the kind of 'And...' I was hoping for, but it IS one that makes me blush.

"Really?" I mouse-squeet in surprise.

"Oh, yes. Mademoiselle Fabienne says you're

a very mature and thoughtful girl. And Miss Amethyst was incredibly impressed with the lesson you taught the Newts. She said the way you inspired them was quite remarkable."

Wow. I've never been called mature, thoughtful and remarkable before. Miss Solomon at my old school is nice enough, but the only thing she'd called me lately was Daisy instead of Dani when she muddled me up with the class hamster.

"As for the students, well, what can I say?" Lulu continues. "The younger ones are all a bit starstruck and desperate to get your attention. Sorry if it's sometimes in the wrong way."

Lulu turns and gives me a wry smile. I guess she's talking about the triplets and the marshmallow incident. Or the fact that they blackened a sliver of their front teeth just to copy my 'look'...

But I guess I've got stuff wrong, too. I haven't tried to talk to Blossom to say thanks for her funny little 'HELLO, DANI DEXTERER' stick message.

"But there is one thing in particular I'd like to talk to you about," Lulu carries on, coming to perch herself on the edge of the desk. "Do you know what I caught Yaz doing after bedtime last night?"

"No," I mumble, feeling a flicker of guilt. What me and Yaz have in common is our plans to get away from St Grizzle's as soon as possible. Has Yaz become more determined to escape because of our chats? Maybe Lulu found her climbing out of the dorm window with her case, a snack-pack and a map to the nearest station...

"I caught her in the kitchen drawing cartoon faces on all the eggs," says Lulu. "Yaz said she

wanted to film them. She said she got the idea
from YOU."

Oh ... am I in trouble?

"And for that, I want to
thank you VERY much,
Dani!" says Lulu earnestly.
"In the last couple of
months, we haven't
managed to get Yaz

interested in ANY of the fun, creative things
we're doing here at the all-new St Grizelda's.
What you've done is quite, quite miraculous!"

So now I'm mature, thoughtful, remarkable
AND quite, quite miraculous?

I'm also red. Very, very red with a ginormous
mega-blush under the gaze of my beaming head
teacher.

KNOCK-KNOCK-KNOCK!

Hurray for the distraction! Lulu smiles at

someone in the doorway, and *SQUOOOOFFFLE
-pffffffffffff...* myself around to see who it is.

"I've got a message from Swan," says Zed,
rolling backwards and forwards as if he's nervous.
"Could she speak to Dani upstairs in the dorm,
please?"

"Sure, I think we're done here," says Lulu,
reaching a hand down to me. I shyly grab it and let
myself be hauled up in one quick move.

"Thank you," I mutter, then follow Zed as he
swivels himself around and heads back along the
corridor, with a quick veer left to avoid slip-sliding
on plastic-drinks-bottle skittles and
cabbage balls that've now been
abandoned by bored
Newts.

"What does Swan want?" I ask him nervously.

All the lovely compliments I just had heaped on
me fade away with every step. After all, Swan is

(whisper this) a tiny bit scary. Is she about to have a go at me for overreacting to the school mascot nibbling some dumb old toy of mine?

"Um, dunno," says Zed, though I think he might have a bad case of the fiberoonies.

We're at the bottom of the grand staircase now, where Twinkle is eating the last couple of leaves left on the remains of the pot plant.

"Got to leave you here," Zed announces with a grin, nodding down at his chair.

"Oh, of course," I say, and begin to tiptoe my lonely way up the carpeted steps, a flump of dread glooping in my tummy.

"Dani?"

I pause and gaze back down at Zed.

"Yaz says you're not going to stay. Is that true?" he asks.

The heart-tugging, puppy-in-the-rain expression on his face makes it too hard to be honest and say "yes", so I just give him a vague, cowardly shrug in reply. Then I quickly turn and head on up to the first floor, the dorm and whatever Swan has in store for me. (Gulp.)

With a heavy heart and heavier steps, I take my key out of my pocket – but the door to the Fungi dorm is already open wide.

And hold on – what's that?

From inside I hear titters and shushed giggles. Is there going to be an audience for my dressing-down from Swan?

"Deep breath, Dani," I tell myself. I step into the room and see a muddle of schoolmates.

There are Otters on the floor and Newts are perched on various top bunks like raggle-taggle rows of sparrows on rooftops.

Conkers hunker on the bottom bunks, including Yaz, who gives me a wave and a you'll-be-fine smile.

In fact, everyone is grinning and giggling, as if secrets might spill out any second.

Then a skinny, scruff-haired goblin leaps in front of me, and grabs my hand.

"LOOK, Dani Dexterer!" yelps Blossom, pointing over to my bunk in the corner, where

Swan sits crosslegged on my duvet.

I gasp. But it's not the sight of Swan that's making me gasp.

It's the giant T rex that's spray-painted on the wall by my bed. Its roaring head nearly touches the ceiling. Its powerful tail trails under the window.

It might be the most **AWESOME** thing I have ever seen.

"It's … it's a sort of sorry," Swan says, wafting her hand towards her handiwork. "Like it?"

"I LOVE it!" I say as I let myself be led closer by Blossom.

"And she did something else!" Blossom says urgently, pointing to something resting in Swan's lap.

Swan offers it up to me and my heart goes squidge. It's my T rex. He has a bandage around his gnawed tail and a lookalike plaster cast on his chewed left leg. There's even a crutch made of twigs and string wedged under his weeny arm.

"He's not the way he was, but I think he can still act," says Swan with a smile that's halfway between cheeky and hopeful. So she knows about my mini-movies? Yaz must've told her.

"Y'know, I think he can," I tell her, taking my

star ex-toy from her outstretched hand.

"And I made you a present, too, Dani Dexterer!" says Blossom, taking something from behind her back and passing it to me. "It's to say 'Happy You're Here'. It's a model of a bird's nest."

I gaze down at Blossom's lumpy gift, which looks like it's been made of mud ... and bits of bird's nest.

"Thank you," I say quickly, and am quickly deluged with claps and whoops.

I glance around at the small and not-so-small girls in the dorm and see nothing but sunshiney smiles.

And in that moment, a hard blue something melts inside me.

"Do you want to come and play bowling downstairs, Dani Dexterer?" asks Blossom as the applause begins to fade.

"Um, in a minute," I tell her, as I realize that one important someone isn't in the room – and that I have a different answer to the question he asked me.

With (just about) the whole school's eyes on me, I hurry out of the dorm and pitter-patter at high-speed down the grand staircase till I reach the hall.

Zed's not there.

But the front door is open ... and now I see that he's over by the statue of St Grizzle's, gloomily throwing coloured hoops at her hands.

I hurry past the hatch to the office, where Twinkle is up on her back legs licking the pages of the visitor's sign-in book while Toshio snoozes at his desk.

Outside, the warm sun is on my shoulders as I run towards Zed.

"Hey!" I call out, waving the hand that's still clutching my precious lumpy mud nest.

"Hey!" Zed calls back, waving a green plastic hoop in return.

"Listen, I've been thinking, and—"

Ding-a-ling-a-ling! goes my phone before I can finish.

"Uh, here," I say, quickly reaching up and putting my recovering T rex and Blossom's present in St Grizzle's handy hands so I that can fish my phone out of my pocket.

Great – it's Granny Viv!

"Hello ... Dani?" says her voice in my ear.

"Hi, Granny Viv," I say with a huge smile. "How's Wales? How's your friend?"

I just realized I hadn't asked before. I've been too wrapped up in how I was feeling.

"Eh?" mutters Granny Viv, sounding momentarily confused. "It's lovely, and Daphne's fine – why do you ask?"

"Because she's been ill, and you went to look after her?" I reply, feeling pretty confused, too.

"Oh, I just told your mother that to make her feel guilty; to show her that SOMEONE appreciated me and trusted me to look after them!" says Granny Viv, with an embarrassed, slightly guilty laugh. "Anyway, never mind that. How are YOU, sweetheart?"

"I am good," I tell her, which I know is going to come as a pretty BIG shock. "In fact, I am better than good. Granny Viv, I've changed my mind. I LIKE it at St Grizzle's. I think I might want to stay!"

Zed's "**WHOO-HOO-HOO!**"s practically drown out what Granny Viv says next.

"Oh, I was dead set against you going to St Grizelda's, of course, but as soon as I saw that new website I was SURE you'd really like it!" I just manage to hear her say. "When you were telling me about it, Dani, I thought it sounded such **TERRIFIC FUN!**"

Everything here IS terrific (crazy, weird) fun. Why didn't I get that till now?

I guess I just didn't allow myself to see how great St Grizzle's really is because I felt like … well, I felt like it meant I didn't love, love, LOVE Mum and Granny Viv and Arch and Downboy and home.

But I think – I know – I can still love them all and be happy here…

WHUMFFF!

I gasp as something clunks into me and I find myself plonked backwards on to Zed's knees.

"HELP!" I shriek.

"You're **STAYYY- IINNGGGG!**" yells Zed, taking us on a victory hurtle down the incline of the driveway to the school.

"Dani? Dani, hold on – I need to tell you someth—" I hear Granny Viv say before we're out of range and the connection cuts out.

A few speeding seconds later, Zed spins his chair round to stop us before we hurtle too far. A few seconds more and we're both still trying to catch our breaths from the speed and the laughing.

"You idiot!" I giggle, pushing myself up off his lap and shaking myself sensible. "I lost my gran there!"

Sure she'll have left a message, I check my phone and yes – there she is. A little dizzy, my fumbling fingers accidentally press the speakerphone button.

"Oops – don't know what happened there..." Granny Viv's voice drifts out as I stare back up the driveway at the grey school building with its painted flowers and bugs and silliness at every window. And there's the statue of St Grizzle, her hands adorned in yellow rubber gloves, and carefully holding my gifts and Zed's hoops, wearing the plastic-spoon crown at a rakish angle on her stone head.

What a great, GREAT place St Grizzle's is...

"...but listen. There's a problem," Granny Viv says urgently. "I know I haven't been, well, TALKING to your mum much since she decided to send you away. But we finally spoke this morning and she's been SO worried about you

– especially with all the texts and messages you've been leaving her – that she's decided to cut her course short."

NO!

"She's found another boarding school and she's coming to take you to see it."

NOOOO!

"Today."

NOOOOOOOOO!

"Hey, don't worry, Dani!" says Zed, who's heard everything, of course. "It'll be all right!"

"Will it?" I ask him, hoping he's got an excellent plan up his T-shirt sleeve.

"Er, I dunno … it's just something people say, isn't it?" he says sheepishly.

Stupid random boy – I'm doomed…

OK, maybe I'm not quite doomed.

Chapter 13
Not Quite Doomed

And some pants...

Zed might've failed when it came to having a plan but luckily he's related to someone frighteningly sharp and smart.

And right now, the frighteningly sharp and smart Swan is tap-tapping her pen against a clipboard as we all stand to attention in the front entrance hall.

"Dorms tidy?" she asks, reading from the Dani's-Not-Quite-Doomed To-Do List.

"Dorms are tidy," says Yaz, proud of her dorm-tidying team of Conkers and Otters.

"Hallways and corridors free of games and goats?" Swan checks next.

"Yes!" says Klara. "The Newts put EVERYTHING away. And I tied Twinkle to the tree in the back garden."

That's good. Mum doesn't need to be welcomed by a rampaging goat when she arrives, which could be ANY MINUTE NOW.

AARRGHHH!

"Everyone clean and in their best clothes?" Swan continues.

"Absolutely," says Miss Amethyst, smoothing her hands over a rather spectacular purple velvet dress and lilac pashmina.

"I meant the kids," Swan snaps, glowering at Miss Amethyst over the clipboard.

"*Oui*, the children are clean and tidy," Mademoiselle Fabienne nods enthusiastically.

"Me, too," says Lulu, who's wearing her smartest jeans, a simple white blouse and hair that's been blow-dried by Yaz. "You know, I still think this is over the top. I'm sure if I just spoke to your mum, Dani, I'd be able to convince her that St Grizelda's is the perfect school for you..."

"Lulu, one word. CLOSURE," Swan tells her own mother sternly.

"But—"

"But Swan's right, Lulu," Yaz bursts in. "You can't afford to have anyone else leave. And as you know, my father is coming for me any time now, so you HAVE to encourage new people to stay, in any way you can…"

Bless her, Yaz might be desperate to go – and is convinced I've gone loopy for wanting to stay – but she's still oddly loyal to St Grizzle's. Accepting that fewer students + less money = St Grizzle's closing, Lulu nods resignedly.

"OK. Last checks," Swan announces.
"Refreshments?"

"May-Belle's made cakes – she's just getting them out of the oven now," I tell her, relieved that the triplets aren't in charge of the catering. Their job was to go out and beautify St Grizzle herself, to make a good first impression on Mum.

That done, they're now huddled by the bottom of the stairs, tying tissue-paper flowers to the bare branches of the pot plant that Twinkle demolished.

"Cool," says Swan, tap-tapping further down the list. "Toshio – can you run through your speech again?"

"Yes," Toshio answers her, giving a low bow that my mother can't fail to find polite. "'Welcome, Mrs Dexter. Please take a seat and I'll let the head teacher know you aren't here.'"

Swan narrows her eyes at him for a second then shrugs. "Close enough."

"Hey, I think I hear a car coming!" says Zed, who's on watch at the front doors.

I think I'm about to faint and so I twist the head of my T rex to distract myself.

Everybody at St Grizzle's has practised being normal all morning, but we probably would've needed several months' worth of rehearsals to make it convincing.

"Yep – car coming up the driveway!" Zed confirms.

"Time to get into position," orders Swan. "Everyone to Miss Amethyst's room, ready for the Newts' performance."

This is good. This is working. The Newts have been in there rehearsing 'The Periodic Table Song' for the last ten minutes. Mum HAS to be impressed by a bunch of eight-year-olds knowing all the chemical elements several years before they're actually taught them in school.

"Yes, well, good luck with THAT!" Mrs Hedges suddenly calls out as she bustles through the back door with armfuls of clean laundry. "The Newts are all out on the lawn and the state they're in, I don't think they're coming inside anytime soon..."

"LOOK WHAT THEY'VE DONE! THEY ATE THEM!" wails May-Belle, tearing from the kitchen with a tray of mostly empty paper cupcake liners.

The three cakes left untouched are ominously black, as if they've been burnt. But on closer inspection, I can see they're not burnt at all. They've just been covered with a thick layer of goth-coloured icing, as Lulu has just noticed.

"Oh dear," she sighs, scooping up one of May-Belle's dark offerings and inspecting just how incredibly thick the icing is. "That is a LOT of sugar..."

"*Zut alors!*" Mademoiselle Fabienne calls out in horror, but the reason isn't anything to do with potential sugar disasters.

She's staring at the triplets, who've just finished fixing up the pot plant and are now obediently waiting to be told what to do next.

Only they're smeared in apple green eyeshadow and powder pink lipstick that looks like it's been applied by a gorilla in a blindfold and boxing gloves.

Uh-oh. I suddenly have a **VERY BAD FEELING** about how the girls have 'beautified' St Grizzle...

"RAAAAGHHHHHHH!"

The roar comes out of the blue or, more precisely, in through the back door.

Y'know, most people find horror movies terrifying. But hide-behind-the-sofa-scary horror movies have nothing on ten eight-year-old girls crazy on sugar and food colouring.

Black icing is smeared around their grinning, growling mouths and every one of them is wild-eyed and wearing pants on their head, newly pinched from the washing line.

"**HOLD IT!**" yells Zed, selflessly steering his

chair towards Blossom and the rest of her careering crew to try and head them off before they get any further into the front entrance hall.

Sadly Blossom assumes he has a completely different something in mind and leaps on to the armrests.

"WHEEEEE!"

"No – get off!" shouts Zed, spinning the chair around.

"I'm **KING OF THE WORLD**!" yelps Blossom, her bare feet on the armrests, balancing like a wobbly baby goblin, her arms outstretched … just as Mum walks in through the open front doors.

There's complete silence for a moment.

Mum stares up at Blossom, then around at her pant-headed girl tribe, the triplets with their clown make-up, the mini-goth clutching her black-splodged baking tray and the somehow-escaped goat that's now chewing on the tissue-paper flowers.

Then I hear a nervous cough.

"Welcome, Mrs Dexter," a bowing Toshio suddenly announces. "Please take a seat and don't be here."

Before anyone can react or correct his English, there's another sound.

It seems that tissue-paper flowers don't agree with Twinkle, and she has just thrown up a multi-coloured lump of them on the grand staircase.

"Mrs Dexter," Lulu launches in, clearly thinking she'd better make the best of this clearly AWFUL situation. "Can I just say—"

But a wobbly little voice interrupts her.

"Oh, helium and hydrogen," sings Blossom, "your daughter Dani taught us all of them!"

There's a pause, then all of the pant-headed Newts join in with the entire 'Periodic Table Song' at high speed.

"Bravo! Bravo!" Miss Amethyst calls out at the end, clapping so wildly that everyone's compelled to join in. "Apologies for the outfits, Mrs Dexter. The girls are … are rehearsing for a play I've written. A comedy, of course."

"Mmm," Mum mutters. "Can I just have a word with my daughter? In private, please?"

Me and my T rex follow Mum outside as she walks towards the car. This is when she tells me to get in and never look back, isn't it?

"Dani, Granny Viv called me before I set off here," says Mum, slowing down and turning to look at me. "She says that now you've got used to St Grizzle's, you've had a change of heart. She says you love it here and that she thinks you'll be very happy. Is that right?"

"Yes, yes!" I babble. "At first … well, I guess I thought I hated it. But then I got to know everyone and saw how brilliant this place is, even if it is a bit mad around the edges."

"So you really think this would work, Dani?" Mum checks with me.

"I do," I say simply, "cos I fit in here!"

And that's the truth.

From smiley Toshio to the staring triplets, from Twinkle to Blossom the mutant goblin, St Grizzle's is full of oddballs and strays. And I'm pretty much a dinosaur-loving, movie-making oddball and a stray, too – at least for the next three months, while Mum's away.

"OK, so can you promise me that I'm not making a GIANT mistake if I let you stay here?" As Mum speaks, I see her frowning over at the statue of St Grizzle, with her smears of green eyeshadow and smudge of pink on her stone-grey lips – the exact same shade of pink as the spotty pair of pants she's wearing on her head.

"I promise, Mum! Thank you!" I say quickly,

giving her a giant hug before she can change her mind and trying not to jab her with the T rex.

"Oh, I do love you, Dani Dexter!" she says, hugging me right back.

"Even more than penguins' bums?" I muffle into her chest.

"Even more than penguins' bums!" she laughs, pulling away to look at me. "So, any chance of a cup of tea before I head off?"

"Definitely," I reply, linking my arm into Mum's as I lead her back towards the school. (I just hope she doesn't expect cake...)

The staff and students of St Grizzle's watch us from the doorway, smiling nervously and trying to figure out my fate.

Sensing from my own broad smile that I'm staying, Zed gives me a relieved thumbs up. Beside him, Swan blows and **POPS!** her bubblegum like a mini celebration.

"But PLEASE tell me you're learning something here, Dani," Mum sort-of-jokes. "PLEASE tell me it's not as silly as it seems..."

"I'm learning stuff and it's not as silly as it seems," I assure Mum, while quickly kicking a cabbage into the bushes.

As we stroll across the gravel, I also spot a trail of small, muddy bare footprints across the top of Mum's car, as well as Miss Amethyst shooing Blossom out from under her long, flowing purple skirt, and a triplet attempting to put green eyeshadow on a very patient Twinkle.

Then – **ping!** – two thoughts hit me at once...

1) never mind my random toy actors – how many views would I get on YouTube if I filmed all this real-life loopy stuff?

2) And how much do I love, love, LOVE that this is just another NOT-normal day at St Grizzle's School for Girls, Goats and Random Boys!

Shhh...
How about a
sneak peek at the
next story in
the series?

GRIZZLE'S
~~ST GRIZELDA'S~~
SCHOOL
FOR GIRLS,
GHOSTS AND
RUNAWAY GRANNIES

And some secrets about
Karen and Becka!

Things Mum is missing in the Antarctic...

   1) me

   2) Granny Viv

   3) Hobnobs

   4) *green*.

"It's so WHITE here!" she said when she FaceTimed me yesterday, turning the phone around so I could see all the snow and ice.

So I'm making a mini-movie especially for Mum this afternoon, featuring a rolling English field and a herd of cows.

Sort of.

Well, OK, so it's a bunch of potatoes on the front lawn of St Grizzle's.

Yaz and Blossom helped by sticking googly eyes on the 'cows' (i.e. potatoes the triplets BORROWED from the school kitchen).

"Yep, that's about right," I say to Klara and Angel, who've been carefully placing the spud-herd on a patch of grass. I'm directing them as I lie on my tummy, holding my phone sideways to film. "And ready to move them again?"

I'm shooting a rehearsal. We'll use proper stop-frame animation for the final version where, bit-by-bit, the 'cows' will meander across the screen.

"Moo!" says Zed, practising the sound effects.

"Excellent," I tell him.

"Uh-oh!" I hear Swan call out. She's watching us from over in the tyre swing.

"Incoming GOAT!"

Before anyone can shoo Twinkle away, four giant legs have got into the frame. First she sniffs at the camera, then at the lead actor potato, before

– **CRUNCH!** – happily munching it between her yellow teeth.

Well, that film's ruined! I think to myself.

I'm about to stop recording, but then I hear ANOTHER sound – my schoolfriends howling with laughter.

So I stay where I am and keep filming.

After all, a giant goat photobombing a herd of tiny potato cows might get me my most popular ever video on YouTube!

Though it's going to be hard to beat the 903 views I got last Sunday when the Newts class decided that eight months was WAY too long to wait till winter and covered the statue of St Grizzle with squirty-cream snow...

Next, Dani will be directing a film for a local competition, which could mean a big prize for her, her schoolfriends AND St Grizzle's!
But will run-ins with the village kids, runaway grannies and ghostly goings-on TOTALLY ruin her excellent plan?

St Grizzle's School for Girls, Ghosts and Runaway Grannies
— coming soon!

Karen McCombie

Karen McCombie is the best-selling author of a gazillion* books for children, tweens and teens, including series such as the much-loved 'Ally's World' and gently bonkers 'You, Me and Thing', plus novels *The Girl Who Wasn't There* and *The Whispers of Wilderwood Hall*.

Born in Scotland, Karen now lives in north London with her very Scottish husband Tom, sunshiney daughter Milly and beautiful but bitey cat Dizzy.

Karen loves her job, but is a complete fidget. She regularly packs up her laptop and leaves Office No. 1 (her weeny back bedroom) and has a brisk walk to Office No. 2 (the local garden centre café).

Her hobbies are stroking random cats in the street, smiling at dogs and eating crisps.

You can find her waffling about books, cats and bits & bobs at...

www.karenmccombie.com
Facebook: KarenMcCombieAuthor
Instagram: @karenmccombie
Twitter: @KarenMcCombie

*Okay, more than 80, if you're going to get technical.

Author Factfile

- **Favourite thing about being an author:**
  Ooh, doing school visits, where I can meet lovely real people, instead of staring at wordies on a computer all day.

- **Second most favourite thing about being an author:**
  Eating cake while I'm writing at Office No. 2 (i.e. my local garden centre café).

- **Best question ever asked during an event:**
  "What's your favourite flavour of crisps?"
  (My answer was ALL crisps are good crisps, but ready salted will always win my heart...)

- **Tell us a secret!**
  Early on at school, I was rubbish at reading and writing because of an undiagnosed hearing problem. From the age of five to six, I basically sat in class wondering what on earth was going on around me. It took an operation and a lot of catching up before I learned to read and write well.

- **Favourite waste of time:**
  Dancing whenever I get the chance, much to my daughter's shame (like THAT'S going to stop me!).

Becka Moor

Becka Moor is an illustrator/author from Manchester, where they say things like 'innit' and 'that's mint, that' when something is really good. She managed to escape the North for a couple of years and ended up in Wales (which, as it happened, was still up North) where she studied Illustration for Children's Publishing at Glyndwr University. Since moving back home, Becka has set up shop in a little home office where she works on all kinds of children's books, including the 'Violet and the Pearl of the Orient' series and *The Three Ninja Pigs* picture book. When she's not hunched over a drawing or pondering which texture to apply to a dragon poo, she can be found chasing her two cats around the house begging for cuddles, or generally making a mess.

You can find more useless information in these dark corners of the interwebs:

www.beckamoor.com

Twitter: @BeckaMoor

Blog: www.becka-moor.tumblr.com

Illustrator Factfile

- **Favourite thing about being an illustrator:**
  Drawing all day!
- **Second most favourite thing about being an illustrator:**
  Getting to read lots of brilliant stories and imagining
  how the characters might look.
- **Tell us something odd!**
  I have a mug collection so huge that the whole world
  could come to my house for tea at the same time, but
  someone else would have to provide the biscuits!
  I'll have a Hobnob or five, please.
- **Favourite waste of time:**
  Baking. It's only a waste of time because I can't bake and
  whatever comes out of the oven is usually inedible!